Unveiling the Duke's Heart
A Clean Regency Romance Novel

Martha Barwood

Table of Contents

Prologue 4

Chapter 1 9

Chapter 2 15

Chapter 3 23

Chapter 4 28

Chapter 5 34

Chapter 6 39

Chapter 7 45

Chapter 8 49

Chapter 9 54

Chapter 10 61

Chapter 11 66

Chapter 12 71

Chapter 13 77

Chapter 14 80

Chapter 15 88

Chapter 16 92

Chapter 17 96

Chapter 18 102

Chapter 19 107

Chapter 20 111

Chapter 21 118

Chapter 22 123

Chapter 23 129

Chapter 24 137

Chapter 25..142

Chapter 26..147

Chapter 27..151

Chapter 28..155

Chapter 29..159

Chapter 30 164

Epilogue 168

Extended Epilogue 173

Prologue

Sunlight shone through the windows in the library onto the settee where a young woman sat reading. She smiled from time to time, enjoying the peaceful afternoon, and being surrounded by her father's many books which he had loved as much as she did now. She eagerly turned the page of Northanger Abbey. It had been written by Miss Jane Austen, one of her favourite authors. Making her pause to wonder what it would be like to have an adventure. Despite this probably not being the most suitable thing for a young lady to do in early June, 1818 but which didn't deter her in the least.

Sophia Barlow had a mind of her own, and privately considered herself to be a bluestocking. It wasn't long before her thoughts returned eagerly to the Abbey, and what would happen next to Catherine, the heroine in the story. Nevertheless however independent she might like to think she was, Sophia had been under her eldest brother's guardianship for the last four years. After their father's sudden death because of a heart attack. This had proved to be a highly unsatisfactory arrangement. Mostly because Lucas had been trying his best to marry her off to a succession of gentlemen during the last twelve months. Despite Sophia being of the opinion that he would eventually lose interest in this, he still hadn't given up.

She sighed to herself. Any one of the gentlemen he had insisted she should consider could easily have qualified as the worst bachelor in the current London season! However, trying to remain optimistic about the future, she continued to hope that Lucas would change his mind. Not realising that it had become increasingly clear to everyone else that he didn't have any intention of doing so, until she had married a gentleman of his choice. Justifying his actions by taking a high moral stance. Often reminding her that it was his duty to look after her well being, now that Papa was no longer with them, and he really did only have her best interests at heart.

Sophia took a very different view of the matter, and couldn't wait until she had reached her twenty-first birthday. When she believed, without any knowledge of the wider world or legalities of her situation, that she would be able to do as she pleased in matters of the heart. Consequently in the meantime she had little regard for Lucas or his opinions, but still tried her best to keep out of his way as much as possible. Remaining determined to marry for love, if she was fortunate enough to find the right gentleman, and nothing Lucas did or said was going to persuade her to the contrary.

Sophia was dismayed when the door of the library was thrown open, and her brother walked in with that horrible smile he used when he was up to something, which would usually be to someone else's disadvantage. Lucas Barlow had no hesitation whatsoever in doing as he pleased. If others didn't like the man he was, or what he did, it was of little concern to him. In his far from humble opinion he had been badly treated by life when he failed to inherit a title on his father's death, and it didn't worry him in the least that he was disliked by the majority of people he came across. If not feared. He also had no hesitation about treating his family in the same way. He enjoyed the ruthless side of his nature a little too much. Whilst being egotistical, and spiteful, came easily to him.

In reality, and irrespective of what Sophia might believe, he was very angry that she had dared to thwart his wishes for so long. He still couldn't understand why she believed she had the right to do so. As the eldest son it was only right and proper that he was head of the family now, with their father's blessing. He also firmly believed that if he couldn't have a title then this shouldn't stop him from becoming very rich, however he had to go about it, and he certainly wasn't prepared to allow his sister to stand in his way.

Lucas glanced around his father's library where Sophia usually spent every available minute of her time. Instead of devoting herself to doing needlework in the parlour, as she ought to. He was fully aware that her infernal love of books was at the heart of her disobedience. Also scribbling those words she called poetry. She had a book open on her lap now! She had clearly been reading it, and even if she did think of herself as one of those ridiculous bluestockings, it was completely unacceptable.

From what Lucas had seen of the debutantes coming out this year, those who were acquiescent and didn't appear to consider it proper to think for themselves, fared much better. He suspected too that the money he had spent in sending her to a finishing establishment, once the mourning period for Papa had passed, had been a waste of time and money. He had hoped that receiving this tuition would result in her changing her ways, to become a much better proposition for a suitor. Someone of his choosing who would help him further his business interests, and quest to become a much richer man than their father had been. Whilst if anything, Sophia had come back more feisty and difficult than before she left.

Lucas stamped his foot in temper. Confound the girl! It was her duty to obey him, and he couldn't wait to pass the responsibility of guiding her onto her husband. It would be an added benefit when he secured a marriage proposal for her. He only had one sister, so one chance at getting the most he could out of matchmaking for her. He had been scouring the London clubs since the start of the season looking for the wealthiest and most desperate men he could find, who would easily succumb to his way of thinking. That in exchange for getting a beautiful young wife immediately, without having to endure the season and its host of ruthless mamas, Lucas would receive an agreed sum of money. Followed by an introduction to his newly found brother-in-law's lucrative circle of business connections.

However due to Sophia's obvious lack of interest in any of the suitors he had selected so far, and wilful behaviour when they met, she had forced him to lower his sights. As well as completely ignoring any of the threats he had made, to get her to comply. Essentially it had now become a case of her marrying anyone who had a title, and more importantly, a large enough fortune who might possibly take her on. Lucas snorted in disgust.

Despite her natural beauty, his sister had made certain that she didn't appear suitably attractive to any of the gentlemen he had introduced her to. Despite the small fortune he had spent on her dressmaker's bills, shoes, and hats.

Hadn't he also made sure that she was presented to Queen Charlotte at the start of the season? Despite her only being a merchant's daughter, and the family deemed by some not to be sufficiently wealthy to be entitled to this privilege. Lucas smirked when he recalled how he had got around that. All it had taken was a word from him in the right ear, and his sister was added to the list of those who had been recommended for presentation to the Queen. Although Sophia had dared to ask him afterwards how he had managed it, and no doubt thought it was somehow connected to his business arrangements, he didn't explain. Why should he? It was enough that he had been able to arrange it, and she ought to be grateful.

Suffice to say that he did have something else in mind for her now. Judging by the look of alarm on her face, she was also aware of it. Not a man to waste words he dispensed with the niceties of asking how she was and said, as persuasively as he could, "Sophia, my dear, a very important business acquaintance of mine will be joining us for dinner in two days' time. I would like you to make a good impression on him. I am giving you sufficient notice of it, so that you will have time to choose the most charming dress in your wardrobe, and do something with your unruly hair." He remarked staring at her light brown tresses, which he still didn't believe she had done her best to style.

Moreover, continually using this lack of attention to her hair as a means of silently objecting to his dismissal of her ladies' maid, shortly after their father's death. Lucas had congratulated himself at the time, believing that the woman was an unnecessary expense. Despite his sister's insistence that she needed a maid to help her dress properly. Thankfully she seemed to have lost heart in making this objection, and even though he was reluctant to admit it, she did look reasonably well groomed now most of the time. Although it had taken her a while to reach this point.

Meanwhile Sophia's hazel eyes flashed defiantly, as she returned her brother's stare, knowing full well that the gentleman

7

to which he was referring would be another suitor. Lucas could also guess by this time what would be going through her mind, and he grabbed the book from her lap, threw it onto the carpet and said, "You will stop wasting your time reading, and do as I ask on this occasion. Showing me you understand the necessity of making a good match before your next birthday." Having dispensed with any subterfuge, he paused to give his next words greater emphasis.

"I expect you to secure a marriage proposal, Sophia. Do you understand me? You will shortly be twenty-one years of age. Far too old then to be considered as a prospect by the majority of decent men, who might be prepared to ignore your bad character and personality. Unless you wish to find yourself out on the street, my dear sister, you will not defy me again."

Lucas glared menacing at her, before he turned around and strode out of the library. Slamming the door behind him as hard as he could, so that the glass ornaments in the nearby cabinet shook. Sophia's face turned pale. Lucas really did mean it this time. She had never seen him so angry before. Maybe her life wasn't an adventure after all. More importantly, she had been wrong in believing that she would be able to marry for love, once she was old enough to choose a husband for herself.

Sophia clenched her hands in despair. If only mama was still here, she couldn't help thinking. Why did she have to die? She would have given her guidance now, and dear papa would never have treated her like this. His marriage to mama had been a love match, so of course she wanted the same. Why was Lucas unable to discern that? All of these circumstances, coupled with the unfortunate demise of her parents, appeared exceedingly unjust.

A solitary tear slid down her cheek. For once, Sophia Barlow felt completely helpless, and didn't know what to do for the best.

Chapter 1

Edward Carlisle yawned as he left his carriage, and walked the short distance to the front door of his late father's townhouse in Belgravia, which had been opened for him by the butler. After greeting Jenkins he gave him his hat, and made his way into the drawing room where he knew that his mother would be waiting for him. It was late, almost eight o'clock, and he assumed that for once she wouldn't object if he didn't change for dinner. After a laborious day managing his business affairs, he was quite fatigued and eagerly anticipated a tranquil supper before retiring early to his chamber. Thankful that despite it still being part of the London season, it would be just the two of them this evening. Not a more formal occasion when they would be receiving guests.

Cynthia, the Duchess of Carlfield, was clearly delighted to see her son and she put her embroidery onto the table next to her as soon as he came into the drawing room. Edward kissed her cheek affectionately, before pouring himself a brandy. Seeing how tired he looked, she decided not to reveal the distressing news she had received earlier until later on. When she asked Ned, as she had called him since he was a boy, he admitted that he hadn't had a lot of time during the day to stop and eat. So he was delighted to agree to them having dinner, without delay. He drank the brandy quickly, and held out his arm to escort the Duchess into the dining room, after she had rang the bell to tell Jenkins that they were ready for dinner to be served.

When a hearty soup had been enjoyed by them both, the bowls cleared away and the main course served, Cynthia couldn't wait any longer. "In truth, Ned, I must impart some disheartening tidings," she uttered, struggling to hold back her tears.

The Duke looked up immediately from his plate of roast beef, potatoes, and Yorkshire pudding. Clearly alarmed after his father's death from an unexpected illness nine years ago, and to whom he had been very close, he tended to fear the worst when his mother became upset. Fortunately, this didn't happen very often. Despite Cynthia Carlisle being almost in her seventh decade

9

and her hair turning grey, he still thought of her as a strong and capable woman. Realising however, especially after how suddenly his father had passed away, that this could change at any time. "I hope you aren't ill, Mama," he said, anxiously.

"No, fret not, Ned. I am quite well, thank you. It is Ruth, my companion, who has caused my distress. She tendered her resignation this morning, and I am at a loss as to how to proceed without her. She was used to my way of doing things, almost like one of the family, and I shall miss her terribly. She was very upset when she had to tell me she would be leaving. Her mother has been taken ill. Naturally she wished to go home as soon as possible to care for her, and her younger siblings."

Edward sighed, inwardly. His mother was understandably very upset. Ruth had been with her for six years, and this couldn't have come at a worse time. They were due to leave London in the next three days for his country seat in Yorkshire, to spend the remainder of the summer there. He had been looking forward to walking through the grounds of his estate again, and the gardens. However the possibility of him being able to enter into a highly lucrative business deal with an acquaintance of his, Lord Watson, had recently come to light. So that it looked as if he would have to travel to France instead, to discuss the details with him, and meet the other gentlemen with whom his Lordship and him would be trading.

Not wishing to cause his mother any further distress or worry, he stood up immediately, with the intention of going to her. Only after she had assured him with great determination that she was indeed well, and commanded him to be seated forthwith to finish his dinner, did he relent. The matter had only been a momentary shock, nothing more.

Assured of his mother's well-being, Edward resumed his utensils and spoke hastily, "Fret not, Mama. If I must journey to France, I shall ensure your company is not forsaken."
I shall make some enquiries tomorrow morning about finding a new lady's companion for you, to replace Ruth. If it isn't

possible to get someone suitable then I shall put off going to Paris for the time being."

"Edward, despite you continually ignoring my opinion that you work far too hard when you don't need to, I can still understand the importance of you entering into an agreement with Lord Watson. From what you told me earlier, it would be extremely advantageous for you to be able to trade in France. Especially after all the trouble there has been the last few years with Napoleon, and his dreadful war. I am assuming that it would be highly beneficial for you to have a friend like Lord Watson who has already established business connections there."

Edward smiled, and tried to make light of the situation without confirming that what his mother had said was right. He would cancel his trip if need be, and he surely would. Also make the enquiries for a replacement companion himself. Even though one of the servants could easily do this on his behalf he wasn't prepared to take any chances that it wouldn't be done to his high standard when it came to looking after his family. Furthermore, he was fully aware what the loss of Ruth must mean to his mother. Cynthia Carlisle was still an independent woman, but the older she had become the less she liked change. Especially after his father's death, Ruth had grown accustomed to the way she liked things to be done. He had often felt relieved that he could leave her in such capable hands when he did need to travel on business.

The Duchess of Carlfield still hosted numerous social soirees, and other events, when they were at the family's country seat. It gave her a lot of pleasure, and, he surmised, a certain amount of pride. She had relied heavily on Ruth to help her with them, and he wasn't prepared to contemplate the thought of her cancelling them because he hadn't found a replacement. Absolutely not! This definitely wasn't a task he could delegate to a servant. Although how he would find someone suitable in such a short space of time he didn't know. Assuming it would be a miracle, if he did.

Meanwhile, even though the Duchess felt much better, now that Ned was at home, she was still reeling from the news. Irrespective of how upset she felt, she had still reacted to Ruth's resignation in her usual sensible manner. Quickly considering the practicalities of what needed to be done, to help the woman who had turned into a friend. At the same time obviously wishing that this hadn't happened. Poor Ruth had been distraught, clearly torn between the two women, but Cynthia had insisted that she must go to her mother. Fully intending to ask Edward to continue paying her servant's wages for as long as she needed the money. She also instructed Jenkins to get one of the footmen to accompany Ruth back to Yorkshire. Making sure he was told to carry her bags, and arrange for the rest of her belongings to be sent to her.

Both Ruth and her had cried, and hugged each other. Ignoring Ruth's insistence that it was improper for the Duchess to do this, Cynthia had replied in her usual matter of fact way that she was speaking complete nonsense, and held her even tighter until she stopped trembling. Completely ignoring the social impropriety of what she was doing. She also gave Ruth her favourite shawl for the journey, and insisted that she had to keep it, which brought a fresh round of tears to her companion's eyes.

After Cynthia had told all of this to Edward over their fresh fruit and ice cream, he wasn't in the least surprised that his mother had done it. In a time when many would not have acted so, she did.
She deserved having someone good and kind to help her. Making him even more determined than before, to find the perfect replacement for Ruth. While Cynthia wished that Ned would also let her help him, he was always the perfect gentleman. Impressing upon her that he was no longer a boy, and it was his duty now to care for her, which had equally made her feel very proud of him. He always tried to appear strong, however tired he might be or unhappy within himself. The reasons for which he hadn't always shared with her, although she had her own thoughts on what might be troubling him, and why she sometimes caught him brooding.

As Edward carried on eating, he was thinking quickly. Wondering what the alternative might be, if he couldn't find a lady's companion at short notice. The Duchess wouldn't of course be entirely alone in Yorkshire. She would have the servants there.

Not all of them travelled to London to spend the season at his townhouse, and they had mostly been with the family for years. Undoubtedly, he trusted Jenkins implicitly, along with his land steward, Tindle. There was also mama's ladies' maid, Florence. He often heard them laughing about something or another when he passed the door of his mother's bedchamber. All of them loved her as much as he did, so he shouldn't feel that any harm could come to her. Nevertheless now that Papa had gone, it was his duty to see that she had every comfort in life.

Again, following his father's example, the servants were also well cared for. Edward made sure personally that their wages were more than enough to cover all of their needs, so that they could in turn take good care of their own families. As far as he was concerned there was little point in being rich unless you could help others, especially those less fortunate. His mother shared this sentiment in the events she organised to raise charitable funds, also in the way she treated others. So much so that his duchy continued to thrive, and there was a part of him which did regret not spending as much time there as he would have liked to. However, Yorkshire held a lot of memories for Edward Carlisle which he still wasn't entirely comfortable with.

He glanced at the Duchess who was cutting the food on her plate into dainty morsels, before popping them one at a time into her mouth. He couldn't help smiling. Despite her elegant appearance, she could be equally formidable when the occasion demanded it. Fiercely defending an injustice, and riding a horse in her younger days like no other woman he had seen. His father had loved her dearly, and he assumed, from a place deep within his heart. Edward sighed, for what might have been. He still missed Papa's deep and reassuring voice at times like this when life seemed overwhelming. Also Joey, his best friend, who had been the Duke of Westling. Neither of them should have died when they did, but he had gradually learned to accept that death was a part of life. Whilst despite Mama's spirit remaining strong, he could also see a frailer side to her now, which hadn't been noticeable before.

Edward knew that it would have given her so much pleasure if he had been able to fill their large house and Yorkshire estate with grandchildren, and for him to have had a wife she could have sat with, treating her as a daughter. Edward sighed more deeply to himself. Making a proposal before now had crossed his mind. He knew that he was considered to be highly eligible by the mamas who followed his every move when he attended a ball, but which he chose to ignore. It seemed to him that unless a marriage had love as its foundation it was a sham, and he wasn't prepared to treat his spouse in that way. She deserved to be loved by him properly. From the little he knew of women, this should be deeply, and passionately. Although he had at one time been prepared to try to do this, he soon realised that he wouldn't have been able to unless he was truly in love. Irrespective of his mother's wishes, that was a moral decision he wished every day that he hadn't had to make.

"I will find you a new companion, Mama!" Edward said, repeating his earlier words, to stop her from worrying that she might not be able to cope without Ruth's help. Also to appease his own guilty conscience, and belief that he had failed her in not marrying sooner.

Chapter 2

Two days later Sophia was in her bedchamber, looking through the small collection of gowns Lucas had paid for in the belief that this would be enough for her to be suitably attired for the season. It was late afternoon, and she had been upstairs since not long after lunch. Ostensibly trying to choose what to wear for dinner tonight, to please her brother and obey his wishes, but in reality writing a nature poem which had distracted her during her walk in the garden that morning. The birdsong, early sunlight, and different varieties of flowers in the small garden had stayed with her. So much so that she knew from experience if she didn't get her observations onto paper the thoughts and poem would be gone. Something which had become an endless frustration for her, since she was unable to regard her time as her own.

There was so much she wanted to explore, and write about, while cautiously appearing not to be interested in anything of the sort in front of Lucas. She had become used to hiding her paper and pen under a cushion when she heard his voice in the hall, or the front door opening if he had been out. Picking up the same piece of embroidery she had been working on since the start of the season, adding only two or three more stitches to it if he came into the room. Thankfully he had so far failed to notice her lack of progress.

She was glad at times like this that her brother had been frugal regarding the number of servants he kept, and hadn't hired a replacement maid to help her dress. At least this meant that she could be alone with her thoughts when she stayed in her bedchamber, and relatively undisturbed. Trusting that the housemaid, Amy, who was of a similar age to herself and sympathetic to her plight, wouldn't reveal the amount of time she spent writing. Least of all to Lucas. The two women had developed a quiet friendship which didn't go beyond the bounds of propriety, but helped both of them to cope in different ways. Sophia spoke kindly when Cook was being unkind, and Amy's quiet voice often made Sophia feel better after Lucas had been spiteful again.

She had spoken to Amy about finding another position, since she wasn't particularly happy being part of Lucas' household. Even though in her heart it was the last thing she wanted her to do. Amy was however adamant that she would stay with Miss Barlow, and not leave her alone. She had seen how much Sophia suffered at Lucas' hands, and dried her tears on more than one occasion. She also did her best to help Sophia with her hair when her arms were tired from struggling with holding the weight of it for too long. Although styling it simply was the best both of them could manage, without any of the bits and pieces of ornament the other debutantes used to intrigue their eligible gentlemen.

Sophia knew only too well that none of this mattered to Lucas. Far better in his eyes that he should continue to accumulate wealth, and keep what he already had. Whereas from what Owen had told her, Papa had left sufficient funds in his estate for all of them to live quite comfortably, without this penny pinching. A disturbing thought came to her then. She hoped neither Mama nor Papa knew what Lucas was doing, as they would surely turn in their graves and not be able to rest easily. Tears trickled down her face again, until she rubbed them away impatiently. This simply wouldn't do! She had left it late enough to choose from the gowns she had already worn many times before, and couldn't delay her decision any longer.

Without further ado she chose the nearest dress from the pile on her bed, and began to brush her hair as the words of the poem came back to her. Determined that they wouldn't be lost, until she pushed them wearily again to the back of her mind. The dress she had chosen was pretty enough, she supposed. White, with sprigs of pale pink rosebuds on the skirt, and ribbons to tie under the bodice. She had certainly been glad to receive it at the start due to not having had many new clothes since Papa's passing. She could wear Mama's pearl necklace with it. This was her favourite piece of jewellery. Lucas had said that she could have the rest of the things Papa had given to her when she was twenty-one. However, as awful as it was, she hadn't completely believed him when he said it. Since he had that strange look on his face. She realised afterwards that she hadn't seen the box the jewellery was

16

in since Papa's passing. It had always been kept on Mama's dressing table, and when she kept on asking Lucas about it, he eventually told her that it must have been lost.

She only had the pearls and coral necklace, since these had been in her bedchamber. Papa didn't have any objection at all to her wearing anything that had belonged to her mother, but she had no idea now what had happened to everything else. Another mystery, she thought, sighing to herself but Lucas would no doubt know the exact whereabouts of the box. With a heavy heart she returned the other dresses to the wardrobe where she had left her two ball gowns. These were made of heavier cloth, and for more formal occasions. Not that she cared particularly about what she wore any more. Especially after hearing two of the other debutantes discussing her lack of dresses, and the shame of not apparently having any new ones. They had attributed this to her lowly position socially, as a merchant's daughter, and to not having a mama to guide her.

Catherine's observations about romance in Northanger Abbey came to her mind in an instant, and the realisation that she completely understood why she had yearned for adventure. Sophia knew only too well by now how it felt to be trapped in a dilemma which didn't seem to have a solution. Unless of course Lucas presented her with a suitor she was drawn to and felt she might be able to love, which seemed highly unlikely. Her other greatest fear, and reason for refusing to accept any of the earlier proposals she had received, was that any one of the gentlemen who had made them might forbid her to carry on reading. Possibly even worse than that, refuse to give her permission to continue writing the poetry she loved. Sophia knew that if this happened her life would truly no longer be worth living, as some gentlemen did expect complete obedience from their wives. Without them ever daring to express an opinion of their own, let alone use their imagination, or think of having an adventure.

Sophia frowned in a most unladylike manner. She couldn't summon any enthusiasm at all for tonight, or their unknown guest. Wishing again that she still had time to put the finishing touches to her poem while recognising the futility of this. Nevertheless she was starting to wonder who their visitor might be, and her optimistic nature dared her to hope again that Lucas had for once invited a gentleman whose company she might actually enjoy.

A short while later, Sophia stepped into the drawing room where Lucas and Owen were engaged in a loud conversation. Their voices were raised, and it appeared to be some sort of disagreement. They stopped speaking as soon as they noticed that she was there. Sophia was alarmed to see the concerned expression on Owen's face when he greeted her. Something clearly wasn't right, and her suspicions were confirmed when the butler announced the arrival of Lord Dilley. Much to her horror, and dismay.

Sophia stared at Lucas, realising that he had tricked her into having dinner with such a horrible gentleman. Taking the chance away from her to plead illness, and need to have a tray brought upstairs to her bedchamber. He had that look on his face again which she equated to someone being about to suffer at his hands, and this time it was going to be her. He was staring at her now, with a mean and hard look in his eyes. A year ago, Lord Dilley had offered for Sophia's hand, and if it hadn't been for Owen's intervention at the time, Lucas would have forced her into an unwanted marriage with him. Owen's persistent defence of her wishes was the beginning of Lucas' stream of suitors being invited for dinner. She had been right in her earlier assumption that her brother was angry. This was his way of seeking revenge on both Owen and her, for daring to argue with him when he was head of the family.

As Owen and her had anticipated, dinner was an extremely awkward affair, with Lord Dilley staring across the table at her throughout in a lewd manner. As she continually rebutted his attempts at drawing her into conversation about inconsequential matters. Being unable to believe her brother had done such a dreadful thing, and not being prepared to make it any easier for her prospective husband. However it was clear that Lucas was enjoying Owen's and hers, obvious discomfort. Whilst they couldn't help feeling relieved when dinner eventually came to an end.

The following morning, Amy knocked politely on the door of Sophia's bedchamber, and told her that she had been summoned by Lucas to have breakfast downstairs with him. Instead of the tray she had asked to be brought to her room. As she stepped into the drawing room, Owen caught her eye and shook his head slightly warning her not to cross Lucas any further. She could also tell by the look on Owen's face that something was very wrong.

Lucas smiled, and told Sophia to take a seat. "Dearest sister, I have some delightful news for you before breakfast is served." He paused, enjoying every minute of her obvious discomfort. "As I rightly anticipated, Lord Dilley has made an offer for your hand in marriage, and on this occasion I have given my blessing to it."

Sophia stood up, immediately after the words left her brother's mouth. "You can't do this to me, Lucas," she said, feeling that the bottom had dropped out of her world.

"But, my dear, you haven't given me any other choice," he replied, in such a way that it would have sounded quite reasonable if it had been concerning anything else.

Owen tried at that point to intervene, expressing his dissatisfaction at the arrangement. Also much to Sophia's surprise, reminding Lucas that she would shortly receive the benefit of the trust fund left to her in Papa's estate. It was a modest sum, but if she was careful she would be able to get by. No longer being an expense that his brother had to pay for. Also since she would soon be twenty-one, there surely shouldn't be any reason for her to be forced to marry against her wishes.

Lucas also stood up then, with two spots of red on his cheeks showing how angry he was. "Owen, I am fully aware of my sister's trust fund, given I am trustee of it, and this really is none of your concern. However, for your information, the majority of the funds were invested in such a way that they received a poor return and what remains is practically worthless."

Owen was clearly very angry when he heard this, also seeing how upset his sister now was, and he demanded an explanation for what he described as the misappropriation of the funds. Suspecting correctly that they had somehow been removed from the trust by Lucas, to find their way into his brother's own pocket. He also mentioned the trust monies his father had wanted him to receive when he was twenty-five years of age, and said that he surmised they had been dealt with in the same way as his sister's.

Lucas had by this time a snide look on his face. Without raising his voice he said, coldly, "You must wait and see, dear brother. In the interim, let us not speak of it further for it does bore me. Pray, sit down and let us take our breakfast as a family.I have already spoken to Lord Dilley this morning. The matter is non-negotiable, and the arrangements are already in hand for your wedding, Sophia. He wishes shortly to travel abroad, taking his new wife with him."

Lucas smiled at her then. "I am sure you will also not have any objection to your husband handling the small amount of money which is left in your trust fund. He will be spending some of his time when you are abroad negotiating business deals with his connections, which will effectively result in both sides of our family becoming richer. The first meeting has been arranged, so you will need to board a ship crossing the Channel as soon as possible. With this in mind, Lord Dilley intends to obtain a common licence so that you can be married by the end of the week.

As soon as Sophia tried to object more strongly, and give an outright refusal to go along with this charade, Lucas reminded her that the situation was entirely of her own making. If she had been more reasonable and considered the other gentlemen properly, whom he knew were interested in her, she could have been happily married by now to the man of her choice.

Sophia began to cry in earnest and Owen intervened again, trying to protect her. "Lucas, that's hardly fair! Sophia didn't have any choice of who would be on your list of eligible suitors. I demand that you reconsider what you are doing. You must know full well that Papa would never have countenanced something as cruel as this, or used Sophia's trust fund to further his own aims. Especially since a lot of the money in it came from our grandfather," Owen said, sadly. Knowing before the words had left his lips that he was wasting his time.

Lucas laughed, as he looked from Owen to Sophia then back at his brother again, before the tone in his voice changed to one which was as cold as ice. "You dare to try and interfere, brother. Accusing me of going against my father's wishes for the family. Let me remind you that I am well within my rights to do this, as your sister's guardian." He cleared his throat before he continued.

"Also to arrange for you to secure a small living in the country as a curate which shall be befitting for your status and, as you rightly mentioned, depleted trust funds which I am again entitled to do. I intend to look into that as soon as Sophia is married. Lord Dilley will be an excellent addition to our family. I am very much looking forward to having him as a brother-in-law. I will not have any more objections to it from either of you. Do you understand me?" He said, glaring at both of them.

"But Lucas..." was all Sophia managed to say before he had turned on his heel with a face like thunder, and strode from the room.

Owen hurried to Sophia's side, and held her as she sobbed. Whispering how sorry he was, and that he would think of something to put a stop to this gross injustice, but without having the least idea what that might be. Also knowing that he would only have a very short time to do it and unconcerned whether or not Lucas would find his behaviour unseemly in comforting his sister like this. As far as he knew he was only doing what his father would have wished while Lucas didn't seem to have an ounce of compassion, let alone love in his body. Owen knew for certain then that he had been right to fear the worst after their father died.

Owen knew that Papa did have doubts about leaving everything in Lucas' control, and this was the reason he had told him about the trust funds. Sadly however, the knowledge was insufficient for Owen to stop Lucas from stealing the money from them. Their father hadn't disowned Lucas when he should have done, because Mama had by this time died and she would never have a word said against her first born son. Sophia had only been eight years old at the time, and Papa let the matter drift. So that even when Lucas began to behave badly, and he doubted him nothing was done about it.

Owen wasn't concerned for his own needs since they were few, but he was exceedingly worried about his sister being married and then under the control of a man like Lord Dilley. Lucas should have had the backbone to help her choose someone suitable. As he would have done, had it been his place to do so. He welcomed the thought of no longer being in his brother's household, or anywhere near him. The stipend would be small, but if he was careful he could manage. Although he was well aware that his own hope of marrying for love and having children would be thwarted, if there was insufficient money to support them all.

"Have faith, Sophia! All will be well," Owen said, gently. Hoping in his heart that it would be so, or that they might have been able to turn back time if fate had been kinder to them. But their father wasn't to blame. Lucas had always been manipulative and difficult, as a child. So that he mostly got his own way, but he had waited until now when he was in a position of strength, to reveal the full extent of his bad character.

All Owen could do was carry on hoping that he would find a way to help Sophia get away from Lord Dilley, and him, before it really was too late.

Chapter 3

Edward's heart sank, as he left the employment agency which he had been told was the best in London. Unfortunately, the agent had said that they didn't currently have anyone available who could replace Ruth. Even worse, it might take two weeks or more to find the right companion for the Duchess of Carlfield. He couldn't stop frowning as he walked. Letting anyone down like this was inconceivable to him. His standards were very high, especially when it came to looking after his family.

Not wishing to return to his office immediately even though his guilty conscience insisted that he ought to be working, he decided to stop at his favourite club near St James' Place for a cup of coffee, and try to read the newspaper in peace. Hoping that this would take his mind off the problem, or possibly give him some fresh inspiration. There might also be someone there who would be able to recommend another agency he could approach.

Thankfully, the club was situated in a side street away from the main road, which had seemed to Edward to be even more noisy and chaotic than usual this morning. In the hustle and bustle of horse drawn carriages, people trying to cross the road, along with the pavement sellers and vagrants. It was a relief when the doorman opened the door to the club, and greeted him by name, stepping aside so that Edward could walk through it into the quiet interior.

He left his hat and cane at the desk, and made his way into one of the smaller rooms where he asked for a coffee to be brought to him. Five minutes later he was sitting in one of the comfortable chairs near the door, with his drink and an unopened newspaper on the table in front of him. His mind was still in a turmoil about what to do next, and whether he should cancel his trip to France, when he was interrupted by a gentleman taking the seat opposite. Edward glanced up at him realising that he vaguely recognised him, but couldn't recall his name.

The gentleman greeted him as the Duke of Carlfield. Placing Edward in an awkward predicament when he was obliged to ask where they had met before, as the man's identity had completely escaped him.

"My apologies for interrupting your reverie, your Lordship," Owen Barlow said politely. "I believe that you did some business with my father, a few years ago. I was with him at the time, albeit a lot younger. However, as we were introduced back then, I was hoping that you wouldn't object to me sharing your table." He glanced around the room which had by this time filled up, then down at the cup he was holding. "I am in desperate need of this coffee, and there doesn't seem to be another seat available. "

"By all means, please sit down, Mr Barlow," Edward replied, as he quickly moved the newspaper to the edge of the table and his cup closer to himself. "I must apologise if I was frowning. It was unintentional. My father used to say even when I was a child that I had a countenance that could terrify even the bravest soul if I frowned. Sadly I am still in the habit of doing it today. Although I do believe that he was only joking." Edward grinned at Owen, and added a further explanation that he did have a lot on his mind which had taken his thoughts miles away. Prompting Owen to nod, and admit that he completely understood. As he was equally preoccupied by a problem.

Edward had taken an instant liking to the young man sitting opposite him, and remembered also that he had later seen his father's obituary in the newspaper. It had saddened him, as in Edward's opinion, he had been an honest and trustworthy man whose integrity was beyond question. Owen too had the same look about him, an open face which invited trust, and a kind manner. Although he did seem to be a little troubled. It wasn't long however before Edward found himself saying that he urgently needed to find a lady's companion for his mother. As he would shortly be travelling abroad on business, and didn't wish to leave her alone on his Yorkshire estate. Despite still being a very capable woman, age and infirmity meant that she could no longer do everything she wished to unless she had some help. Without the benefit of a daughter or daughter-in-law, she was also in dire need of female company at home. He gave a bittersweet smile to Owen, expressing the thought that if Mr Barlow had a sister he was certain he would understand the Duchess of Carlfield's need for female conversation, and someone with whom she could follow more gentle pursuits.

Owen couldn't believe his ears, and thought at first that he must be mistaken. As soon as he realised that he wasn't, he decided to seize the opportunity without further ado. Preceding it with another apology about not wishing to appear bold, he told Edward that he completely understood his mother's need for a companion. Also that he did by chance have a sister whom he believed would be a suitable candidate. Adding that Sophia was well educated, had attended a finishing establishment to prepare her for the season, and was passionate about helping others. Carefully omitting any explanation of her need to escape from the horrendous situation Lucas had put her in.

As it turned out the solution was even better than Owen could have dared hope for. He realised this when Edward told him that the Duchess would shortly be returning to the family's country seat in Yorkshire. This meant that Sophia would have the opportunity to leave London very soon, if of course the Duke decided to employ her. Owen couldn't help thinking that Edward did genuinely seem interested in giving her the job. Especially when he went on to say that if Sophia would be happy to accompany his mother on her journey north, could she come for an interview the following day? It was much to the relief and satisfaction of both of them when Owen agreed on Sophia's behalf that he would accompany her to Edward's town house in Belgravia, at eleven o'clock the following morning, and the arrangement was made.

Edward left the club, with a much lighter heart than when he first went in. Believing that if Miss Sophia Barlow was anything like her brother, and he had no reason to doubt she wouldn't be, he had unexpectedly found the solution to his problem. Owen hastily consumed his coffee, eager to make his way back to his abode and impart the news to Sophia.

He wasn't in any doubt whatsoever that she would much prefer to join Lord Carlfield's household, albeit as a ladies' companion, than become the wife of Lord Dilley who was a truly vile man.

Even though it wasn't in Owen's nature or character to be unkind, or unjust to anyone, he couldn't bring himself to call either Lucas or him a gentleman. Given Sophia's refusal of Lord Dilley's earlier proposal and the cold manner in which she treated him at dinner last night, it must be perfectly clear to his Lordship by now that he was about to marry a beautiful young woman against her wishes. Whilst as far as Lucas Barlow was concerned he might bear the title of gentleman, but that didn't mean he was anything like it at heart. Sophia deserved so much better than to be connected to either of them!

Owen's thoughts turned then to Edward Carlisle. The kindness in his eyes, and voice had impressed him very much. In particular when he spoke of his mother, it was clearly from a place of love and respect as he was fully prepared to lose a valuable business contract, if he couldn't replace her companion with someone suitable before he was due to leave for Europe, rather than let her down. The contract was clearly of no consequence to him when it came to a choice between his mother's welfare and it. He was exactly the sort of husband Lucas should have been looking for on behalf of Sophia. The Duke of Carlfield was obviously very rich. However Owen also surmised that the fact he was a true gentleman meant he wouldn't be prepared to associate himself with Lucas, and his dubious dealings. So the two were unlikely to have met.

Nevertheless, that could easily pose another problem for his sister in the future. If Sophia could be rescued from having to marry Lord Dilley, and subsequently found a suitor who was a gentleman who might even have a title, would he be prepared to marry into a family which had a man like Lucas at its head? Something which could result in disgrace by association at a later date. However Owen looked at it, only a very courageous and honourable man might be prepared to take the risk of marrying Sophia because of Lucas. Whilst for her Owen knew it would need to be a love match. Since she thought love was the most precious thing in the whole world.

He was glad that Edward had to leave promptly to return to his office, and hadn't asked for news of their father. This question could easily have led to him being obliged to mention Lucas, and the possibility that Edward might no longer be interested in meeting Sophia. Lucas' name was tainted throughout the city. He was thought of in many quarters as a scoundrel.

Nevertheless, providence had been on Sophia's side that morning, and Owen Barlow was smiling when he left the club. Intending to make the long walk back to the town house, as quickly as he could, and tell her the good news.

Chapter 4

Meanwhile, Sophia was walking through Hyde Park with her best friend. Miss Hannah Audley. She was the daughter of a baron, and lived a much more comfortable life than Sophia did. So she had instructed her maid, Lizzie, who was walking behind the two ladies to also bring a parasol for Miss Barlow. Lizzie was enjoying being outside in the sunshine, and seeing the myriad of flowers they walked past. It was a glorious day, but Sophia and Hannah were distracted by the latest development in Lucas' attempts at matchmaking on behalf of his sister. Whispering beneath their parasols as they walked, so that the maid wouldn't be able to overhear their conversation.

Hannah was understandably shocked when Sophia told her what Lucas had done and how she had hoped, quite innocently, that he might actually have found a decent suitor on this occasion. Instead of arranging for her to be married in a few days' time under a common licence of all things, so that Lord Dilley and her could leave immediately afterwards for Europe.

"But Sophia, that is absolutely shocking. I suppose you already know that Lord Dilley is as bad as Lucas. It is well-known across the ton how desperate he is to wed, and have an heir for his vast fortune. However his appalling manners and behaviour have deterred even the most   persistent mama from encouraging a proposal from him. When he has ignored this state of affairs and made one, it has always been refused. Even by those debutantes who are themselves in danger of being left on the shelf, due to advanced age or a distinct lack of beauty. I have even heard papa refer to him as an old rogue." Hannah glanced at Sophia who had by this time paled, and joined her in a sharp intake of breath. Both of them duly horrified, by the thought of being forced to marry a man like that.

"I don't know if I should tell you this, Sophia, but I had the misfortune to dance with him a few weeks ago at Lady Forrester's ball. All I can say is that he was extremely rude, and uncouth.

Certainly not a gentleman. Not at all like your brother, Owen," Hannah said, blushing.

"I am sorry to say that he held me far too close when we danced. Something which I'm sure you'll understand I thought could be exciting, if done by the right gentleman, but certainly not Lord Dilley!" Hannah wrinkled her nose in distaste and hesitated. Uncertain, only for a moment, whether she ought to tell her friend the worst part of all this. Especially since she was talking about the man who would more than likely shortly become Sophia's husband. Nevertheless, sheer indignation compelled her to repeat the rest of her story in a much louder voice, which Lizzie was delighted to listen to.

"He then had the audacity to squeeze me, just before the dance ended. Making me feel as if he had taken a liberty, and been far too intimate. When I hadn't given him any encouragement whatsoever. I'm sorry, Sophia. Maybe I shouldn't have told you that, but you cannot possibly marry a man like him!" She paused again, and said more forcefully, "what about your bridal gown, and clothes for Europe? There won't be enough time to have them made." Hannah's last words were filled with dismay.

Sophia shook her head sadly. "I'm afraid Lucas has no interest whatsoever in what I shall wear, or that he has turned what should have been one of the best days of my life into the worst. Not forgetting to mention of course that it will clearly be a disgrace. I shall be pitied throughout polite society, and shunned by the ladies of the ton wherever I go. It's a nightmare from start to finish, Hannah. It will ruin everything. I don't even know if Lord Dilley will allow me to carry on reading, and even more importantly, writing my poems! How shall I survive if I am unable to do so?"

Sophia began to cry quietly then. Much to Hannah's concern. She quickly passed a lace edged handkerchief to her friend, so that she could dry her eyes as they were already receiving curious glances from the passers by. Her maid who was still walking behind them was however delighted. She had gathered enough delicious snippets to repeat in the servants' dining room later which would entertain them all, and it appeared that Hannah still hadn't finished.

"I know I have said it before but I simply can't believe that even Lucas would do such a dreadful thing to you, Sophia. All for money. When, from what you say, he already has more than enough. I know that he is your brother, but he really is the most appalling man! I wish there was something I could do to help you. My life is so different to yours, and for which I can only be very thankful." Hannah touched her friend's arm in a gesture of sympathy. Realising that her words were pointless. There was nothing she could do to help her.

"I sometimes wonder how Lucas became so awful," Sophia said, philosophically. "Mama and papa treated all of us in the same way when we were growing up, but he always had to be the best and win any of the games we played. Owen and I were a lot quieter. Not worrying about such trifles. All we wanted to do was enjoy ourselves. Although I have started to wish now that I could run away. I honestly can't see that I have any other option, if I am to avoid marrying Lord Dilley."

Hannah stared wide-eyed at her friend, and asked anxiously where she intended to go. Finding it difficult enough to believe that something as horrendous as this had happened, without Sophia doing something she had only read about in books.

Sophia sighed, and said quietly, "that's the problem. I have absolutely no idea. I have stopped thinking about trying to outwit Lucas as if it was a game or some sort of adventure I imagined having after reading Northanger Abbey. I am very much afraid now that the reality of the situation is much more unpleasant, and there really is nothing I can do but accept my fate."

Not knowing what else to say to each other after that, they walked on in silence for a few minutes. Until Hannah said that it might be a good idea if they returned home. Sophia was clearly still very upset, and they were drawing a lot of unnecessary attention to themselves. The last thing she wanted to happen was to find themselves in the scandal sheets the following day. When Sophia nodded in agreement Hannah told her maid to hurry back to the carriage, and ask the coachman to collect them from one of the other entrances to the park which was nearby. This meant they wouldn't need to retrace their steps. Lizzie did as she had been told, glad to be able to walk by herself through such a beautiful garden, and imagine that she was also a lady.

Hannah and Sophia waited under their parasols and the shade of the trees holding each other's arm in silent sympathy, and which they continued to do on the drive back to Lucas' townhouse. Neither of them wished to let go of the other, as the threat of this happening permanently in the next few days loomed closer by the second. Although it hadn't been said, both of them had by now realised that Sophia's marriage might well mean their friendship from childhood would soon be over. Something which neither of them wished to face up to, as the mere thought of it was unbearable.

They had only just alighted from the carriage, and gone into the house, when Owen came through the door of the parlour. He was breathless from walking quickly, and pleased to see his sister was at home. Although he tried his best not to be in the circumstances, he was even more delighted that Miss Hannah Audley was with her. He blushed as he greeted them both. Sophia also didn't fail to notice the way Hannah looked at him when he was bowing politely. Since he was afraid of being overheard, or that Lucas might interrupt their conversation, it wasn't long before Owen suggested that if they were sufficiently rested after their walk that morning it would be wonderful to go to Gunter's tea shop in Berkeley Square for ices. The ladies could sit comfortably in the carriage to eat theirs, if the coachman stopped under the canopy that the branches of the plane trees made.

When they were safely in the carriage with Owen sitting opposite he told Sophia again that he was sorry Lucas had behaved so badly, that he hadn't told her about the trust fund, and he would be very concerned about her welfare if she married Lord Dilley. He explained then that he had invited them to leave the house, because he didn't want their conversation to be overheard.

"Thank you, Owen, from the bottom of my heart. Unfortunately I can't see what else can be done, or that I have any choice in the matter," she said, sadly, while Hannah held her hand and squeezed it gently.

Owen's response was not however as either of them had expected. His face broke into a boyish grin. "Oh, but I think you do, Sophia!" He went on to repeat his earlier conversation with the Duke of Carlfield, and that he had arranged for Sophia to go for an interview the following day. He finished by saying that he wished he could have done more. Nevertheless there was a very good chance that it would save her from ending up in Lord Dilley's clutches.

Hannah was clearly delighted, and couldn't help remarking on how clever Owen was to have done this. Whilst also finding his protective matter quite wonderful, although she thought it improper to tell him this. "Sophia, you must do as Owen says. This is your chance to escape," she said, as enthusiastically as she could. Fully intending to do what she could to support him in what she believed to be a highly courageous attempt to save his sister.

Sophia looked from one to the other of the two people she loved the most, and realised that if she wished to save herself from a loveless marriage then this really was what she had to do. "Thank you, Owen," she said, breathlessly. Wondering what she was letting herself in for, and by this time more than a little afraid. Mostly about defying Lucas. Especially if he discovered what she was intending to do before she could escape, and what might happen to Owen if he learned of his part in it.

Later that evening, Sophia joined Lucas and Owen in the dining room for dinner. Her forthcoming marriage to Lord Dilley wasn't mentioned by any of them. Until Lucas remarked smugly over dessert how pleased he was to see that she had finally accepted his decision, and he appreciated her obedience. Reiterating that he did know what would be best for her, and the connection with his Lordship would indeed broaden his business connections considerably.

Sophia didn't reply, but glanced at Owen who gave her a reassuring look.

Chapter 5

Meanwhile Edward's valet was helping him dress for dinner. The Duke had washed and shaved, then put on his favourite blue silk waistcoat and William was in the process now of tying the matching cravat neatly around his neck. Something which Edward didn't always have a lot of patience for, but his mother was expecting guests this evening so it was important that he looked well groomed. Remaining deep in thought about the future was a hindrance, and meant that he wouldn't have paid a lot of attention to his appearance without William's help. Even when the valet had finished the cravat and was helping him into his jacket, before brushing the back of it to capture any stray hairs on the woollen fabric, Edward couldn't stop thinking about how fortuitous his meeting Owen had been for both of them. Fate had definitely been on their side!

All he hoped now was that Miss Barlow would be able to fit into the role of lady's companion for his mother. He didn't actually know if she had any prior experience of this, but assumed that Owen would have mentioned it if she did. Moreover, when would she have had the opportunity to do this? She attended a finishing establishment immediately before her first season, and was still very young. Edward realised then that he should have asked for more information about her, and not get so carried away by the opportunity to solve his problem. A lot would also of course depend on the Duchess, who was quite capable of making her own mind up on matters such as this.

As soon as he had joined her in the drawing room to wait for their guests to arrive, and told her what had happened, Lady Carlfield insisted quite firmly on being present at the interview. Trying her best in the meantime to discover any other snippets of information concerning Sophia, and was deeply disappointed when Edward didn't know any more than he had already told her. Although when she had reflected on this later, his negligence didn't come as any surprise to her. Due to a lifetime of being married to Edward's father and raising his son, she was fully aware that gentlemen weren't quite as interested in social niceties as ladies, who learned the skill of describing the minutest details to each other from a young age.

However Cynthia was very excited to learn that Miss Barlow would be joining them the following morning for her interview, and could barely sit still once she knew this. Much to Edward's frustration, she also continued to surmise this and that about her which she tried her best to get him to confirm. He remained adamant that he didn't know a single thing more about Miss Barlow and a part of him was wishing now that he hadn't mentioned it at all. Until he saw how much his mother was enjoying herself, and tried to be a little more indulgent. Realising just how worried she must have been about coping alone with all of the social events she already had in her diary.

If truth be told Edward was by now almost certain that he would appoint Sophia, and felt instinctively that meeting her would be more of a formality than anything else. Not only was she the answer to his problem, but Edward had convinced himself that she would most likely be the female version of her brother who was a true gentleman. Given how highly Owen seemed to hold her in regard. Having his sister's welfare at heart in making the arrangement for her interview, and stating that he would accompany her himself.

The only question mark so far, as he was concerned, was whether she would make a good impression on the Duchess once they finally met. Despite her enthusiasm tonight, Edward was well aware that she could be quite particular about the way she wanted things done. If Miss Barlow showed that her temperament was similar to his mother's and she wasn't quite as compliant as he had hoped, then things might not work out after all.

However it wasn't long before Jenkins came into the drawing room to announce the arrival of their guests: Edward's aunt Grace, cousin Beatrice, and the gentleman she was betrothed to. Cynthia remained seated, feeling more than a little worn out by all of the excitement earlier, but was soon engrossed in conversation with her sister and Beatrice, Grace's daughter. Leaving Edward, who had stood up immediately to greet their guests, free to talk to Oliver.

Not wishing to risk losing her to someone else, the Duke of Setterton had made a formal proposal at the start of the season for Beatrice's hand in marriage. As Setterton was near to Edward's estate, the two men soon began to discuss current events in their locality.

Dinner was served before long on hand-painted Sevres plates which had been a wedding present to his parents years ago, and still looked stunning in candlelight. Edward made a toast in honour of the happy couple as it had been impossible for him not to see the way Beatrice and Oliver looked at each other. He felt in no doubt whatsoever that they were deeply in love. Reminding him again of his wish to experience this, as well as the necessity of finding a wife as soon as he could. Strangely enough at that precise moment, his Aunt Grace asked him when he was intending to settle down.

Cynthia came quickly to her son's rescue. "Grace, you may pose that question to Ned as many times as you wish, but I doubt he shall provide an answer until he is prepared to do so,."she said to her sister trying to save him the embarrassment of concocting a reply. "I would love to know the answer, but the truth is that Ned is far too busy overseeing his business affairs. However his father would have been very proud of his success, as I am, and I am sure he will wed when the time is right! Pray, do tell me all the particulars of Beatrice and Oliver's upcoming nuptials. What arrangements have been made since our last encounter?"

Edward had meanwhile cleared his throat, since he wished to answer the question for himself. Much to Cynthia's surprise, and delight. As in her opinion it showed that he was at last thinking about finding a wife. "I must admit that I am still enjoying being a bachelor," he said. "But I am encouraged by the proposal Oliver so gallantly made for your hand, Beatrice. For that reason I will admit that it must be my turn next."

Edward was obliged to undergo a lot of teasing after that, and guessing from the ladies about who his bride might possibly be. Whilst Edward could see the sympathy in Oliver's eyes. He had also clearly been subjected to this, with the questions being modified to suit Beatrice and his circumstances.

Edward looked fondly around the table at his family. What he hadn't revealed was that he also wished to marry for love, as his parents had done. So he could only hope that if fate had anything to do with it, the right young lady would shortly come along whom he could fall in love with. Not being quite brave enough to say it though, and endure a barrage of further questioning from the ladies. Knowing full well that they wouldn't give up until he had contributed something more for them to talk about, which he couldn't do. Since there was absolutely no one whom Edward Carlisle could think of that he might even possibly fall in love with.

He tried hard then not to listen to his guilty conscience, telling him again and as often as it could, that he had let his mother down for long enough. Through failing to give her the company and other benefits of having a daughter-in-law, and grandchildren, which she had every right to expect. Edward knew that this guilty feeling was the only reason he might succumb, and make a proposal. Even if it was to someone he didn't, nor believe he could, love. If only he could have enjoyed the London season, its balls and other entertainment, but it wasn't in him to do so. Much preferring the quietness of his Yorkshire estate, and being left to his own devices, although his mother did her best to make it more lively whenever she could, which made him smile.

His feelings about the ton certainly weren't directed at her or any other members of his family. However he was filled with unease by all this endless parading of young women by their ambitious families, many of whom looked as uncomfortable as he felt. Not forgetting those awful scandal sheets which could destroy any decent man or woman's reputation and destiny very quickly. Along with all the unnecessary gossiping which was done, and had become a source of entertainment to those who participated in it. To the point of being malicious and destructive, as far as he could see. Truly, it was all utter nonsense! A sentiment which he knew was shared by a lot of the other gentlemen at his club.

Edward smiled broadly then at how judgemental he had become, but soon reverted to his usual demeanour. Marriage was a serious matter, not only for himself! As the Duke of Carlfield he was considerably more fortunate than those debutantes whose families forced their hands. Compelling them to marry gentlemen who weren't of their choosing, which must have led to a miserable life. Why on earth had love become so complicated, he asked himself? The answer came quickly. It seemed to him that the ways of the ton, and society had made it so. Not nature, or our own inclinations. As far as he could tell, love was a thing of beauty, to be treasured. He knew now that he had the first inkling of this with Felicity until fate had intervened. Since then, it was in the way he had seen others look at each other.

The Duke's thoughts returned to Miss Sophia Barlow. He hoped once again that she would be suitable, and he could ask her tomorrow morning to join his household.

Chapter 6

The following morning when Sophia woke up, she felt very anxious about the future. Also exhausted, as she had been wide awake for most of the night. Only falling into an uneasy sleep when she heard the blackbird singing in the tree outside her window, and realised that it was dawn. Owen's plan for her escape was all she could think of. Even worse what would happen afterwards to not only herself, but also to Owen, whom she loved dearly and wouldn't want to see hurt at any cost.

Lucas would obviously be very angry when he discovered that she had left without his permission. He would know straight away she had done it to thwart his plan for her to marry Lord Dilley. What if he assumed correctly that Owen had helped her? Lucas was not a man to be crossed! That was even assuming Lord Carlfield liked her sufficiently, to appoint her as his mother's companion. Would he really like someone like her whose interest was mostly in reading books, and writing poetry? Not something which young ladies were always encouraged to do by their fathers or husbands. So an employer who was a gentleman would likely be the same. Especially when it stopped them from thinking about the latest fashion, their appearance, and the importance of socialising.

She had to remember not to talk too much about her writing during the interview. This was when she appeared most passionate, which was something else that might go against her as being unseemly. She would need to talk instead about what she had learned at finishing school, which would hopefully be to her advantage as a ladies' companion.

Even if the plan worked and she reached her twenty-first birthday, Lucas was still the trustee of her fund, or perhaps she ought to say the little which it now contained? If she applied to take any money from it, and she would be entitled to, he could find out where she was living. What if he found her instead before her birthday? Even though it wasn't too far away, there was still enough time to look and create a scandal over her disappearance. Even involving Lord Carlfield who would have become unwittingly involved in this sorry affair. There were so many unanswered questions, the answers to all of which frightened her enormously.

Nevertheless one thing she could be certain of was that Lucas' anger would not have any bounds, and be like nothing Owen or her had seen in the past. These unpleasant thoughts, and others she couldn't specifically recall in the morning, remained tangled in her mind throughout the night. Until she had seen Owen and herself thrown out of the family home for their disobedience. Ending up like those unfortunate people who wandered the city streets begging for a coin or scraps, simply to survive.

After Amy had brought her tea and opened the curtains, Sophia got out of bed and looked at her reflection in the looking glass. Frowning at herself, and how dreadful she looked. Her eyes were bloodshot and puffy. Whilst her long hair was tangled and in knots from all of the tossing and turning she had done during the night. She realised then that she would have to pull herself together, and try to stay calm. Lucas didn't have any idea of her plan to leave so nothing had as yet effectively changed. Apart from the need to be sensible and strong, which meant staying in control of herself. As it was vital she made a good impression on the Duke if she truly wanted to save herself from an unwanted marriage, and she most definitely did.

She shuddered at the thought of being Lord Dilley's wife, and the necessity of even being polite to him. Let alone having his hands touching her. No! This wouldn't do. He was as bad as Lucas, but in a different way. The only chance she had of getting through this would be to block all thoughts of her situation from her mind, and try her best to focus on the interview without worrying. Starting with her hair, she thought, as she picked up the brush to begin sorting it out. While she considered the equally pressing matter of what to wear. Knowing full well that the manner in which she was dressed would contribute to the impression she made.

Appearing too frivolous in a dress that was merely pretty probably wasn't the best idea, but one that was more formal might make her come across as too serious and foreboding. Maybe having so little choice from the few dresses she owned would be a blessing in disguise this morning, as tiredness had made her slower than usual in getting dressed. Until it eventually came to her that she didn't really have a choice, so there was no need to think about it any further, and delay going downstairs for breakfast.

She pulled the dress she thought of as her best one from the wardrobe, and stared at it reasonably satisfied. It was her favourite shade of blue, made of a slightly heavier cloth than the others. The bodice wasn't too low cut, and trimmed in a slightly darker shade. She could also wear mama's coral necklace. It was beautiful, and always made her feel closer to mama when she wore it. She adjusted her hair which was again done in a simple style, checked that her bonnet was ready to put on before she left for the interview, and her appearance in the mirror again before she went downstairs feeling satisfied that she had done the best she could on her own, without the benefit of a maid or her mother's guidance. Not realising though the change in her, and how she had dressed, would raise her brother's suspicions.

Nevertheless as she was walking into the dining room Sophia still felt her stomach twisting into knots. Especially when Lucas did look at her suspiciously, and she realised that it would have been better to put the coral necklace on after he had left the house. Maybe also left some of the tangles in her hair, so that she didn't appear quite as well presented, but it was too late now for regrets. Trying to look calm, and less self-conscious than she felt, she sat down in her usual chair.

"You look rather dressed up this morning," Lucas said immediately, without asking after her health and whether she had slept well. Although he often dispensed with politeness when addressing Owen or her. As if this was beneath him, and inconsequential. The question he asked next came out as an accusation. "You are clearly going somewhere on an errand of your own, if I'm not mistaken. I would have remembered if I had told you to do something for me. So where might that be?"

Sophia's heart sank, as she tried to stop the fear she felt from showing in her eyes. Everything depended now on the answer she gave to Lucas, as he could easily forbid her to leave the house. Something which he had done from time to time in the past when he wasn't satisfied with her behaviour, and she had displeased him. She glanced quickly at Owen before replying, but the only

41

thing she could think quickly of saying was that she was going shopping with Hannah.

Lucas laughed scornfully, unable to resist the jibe that she wasn't being entirely truthful. Causing Sophia's heart to miss a beat. Until he reminded her that she didn't actually have any money of her own with which to buy anything, and he certainly didn't have any to waste on frivolity. So she ought to have said that she was accompanying Hannah in her father's carriage, to watch her spending his money on shopping. Lucas seemed very pleased with himself to have made what both Owen and Sophia thought was such a ridiculous observation.

He smiled at Sophia then, and said, "no doubt this situation will be an opportunity for you to change your opinion of Lord Dilley. Since I assume you will shortly be able to spend some of your husband's money, if of course he is sufficiently pleased with you. He will want you to have more gowns and jewellery than I can afford to give you. Maybe this will make you realise, sister, how wrong you have been in questioning my choice of husband for you. When I was only doing my duty and looking after you!" Without feeling the need to say anything else, apart from having business matters to oversee, Lucas left the table.

Owen told Sophia then how beautiful she looked, as he served her breakfast from the dishes on the side table. Wishing she had a good breakfast before she faced the day ahead. He also asked after her health, looking at her face with concern, and told her very quietly not to worry. All shall be well. The Duke was a gentleman, and certainly not someone to be feared. He also knew their brother's plans for the day. Lucas would shortly be leaving the house to meet someone at his club. So he would be gone soon, well before Hannah's arrival.

Owen knew that Sophia had already arranged for Hannah to take her to the Duke of Carlfield's residence. Meanwhile, he was going to leave the house before them, with the intention that they would meet up again in Hyde Park. He would go for now into the drawing room until Lucas left, and suggested that Sophia wait for Hannah in her bedchamber after she had eaten. Believing that if she was out of sight this would be the safest option. Similarly by removing himself to the drawing room wouldn't give Lucas any further grounds for suspicion that something he wouldn't approve of was afoot.

As it turned out everything did go according to Owen's plan, and Hannah arrived shortly after both of Sophia's brothers had left the townhouse. During the carriage ride, Sophia was feeling afraid again, and extremely nervous. Hannah tried her best to make light of the situation reminding Sophia that she was well read, highly intelligent, and a wonderful person. Like Owen she was confident, and had no doubt whatsoever, that her best friend would make an excellent impression on the Duke. She also complimented Sophia on how beautiful she looked, and told her that the coral necklace had been the perfect choice.

Unknown to Sophia she had brought one of her own to give to her, in case she needed it. Appreciating how little she actually owned because of Lucas' penny pinching, but she saw the love in Sophia's eyes when she touched the coral beads which she often did. Hannah realised then that this must make her feel closer to her mother. She decided not to say anything about her own necklace, and Sophia did look beautiful. She hadn't simply said it to make her feel better.

However Hannah desperately wanted to say something else to reassure her. So even though they had spoken of it many times in the past, as young girls do in dreaming about their future husbands, she said, "I believe with all my heart that what you are doing will be for the best, Sophia. Please don't worry about it. I have been thinking a lot more about love, and back to all of the conversations we had about the famous poets. Remember the verse they wrote about love, and Jane Austen's books. They were right, and so are we. Holding up love as the best thing to want in a marriage, and our lives. Lucas can't have any love in his heart to have done this! You are perfectly right to have found a way to avoid spending your life with a man you don't love. Nor is it likely that you'll grow to, because of your dislike for Lord Dilley which I completely understand."

"Hannah, thank you so much. You are my oldest and dearest friend. I only hope I can please the Duke of Carlfield enough for him to employ me, and remain hidden on his Yorkshire estate at least until my birthday. It never once crossed my mind that I would one day be applying for a job as a companion. I'm afraid now that I may not be well suited to it. Nevertheless I shall try hard. Maybe if his mama is sufficiently taken with me she will be happy for me to carry on being her companion, despite the subterfuge, if and when it comes to light. As it surely must eventually. I appreciate it will be a lot to ask the Duke and her to do, but I can't see any other way to escape from Lucas. Now, or after my birthday.

I hope that this will also give us the chance to see each other again, one day in the future." Sophia said, pausing since her voice had filled with emotion. "I can't bear the thought of not seeing Owen or you, ever again!"

The two young women clutched each other then as Sophia tried hard not to cry any more, but accept her situation as dire as it might be. Until Hannah said firmly, to disguise her own doubts, "we shall, Sophia. We must!"

Their conversation was interrupted not long afterwards by the arrival of the carriage at Hyde Park. As arranged Owen had found a quiet place to wait for them, and he climbed discreetly into the carriage as soon as the coachman had stopped the horses.

The light from the smile which Hannah gave him lit her eyes when he took the seat opposite, and he returned it warmly with his own.

Chapter 7

Meanwhile Edward was sitting in his study, busily writing in his ledgers. It was a traditional room, lined with panelling from the Elizabethan era. Sunlight poured in from the garden, through the diamond panelled windows in which the glass was mostly original. The desk Edward sat behind was large, It had belonged to his father. He shared his love of oak furniture, and the tradition which had always been acknowledged by Papa that what he had would one day belong to his son.

Edward felt a pang of guilt again, as he recalled him saying this when he was a small child, to whom the desk seemed overly large and daunting. Even more so now that he hadn't yet been able to produce his own heir to the Carlfield fortune, one whom he could pass onto all that he had in this lifetime. Carrying on the family tradition. Not yet having an heir made him wonder sometimes why he continued to try so hard at building his business affairs. Until something deep inside reminded him that he would have a wife, and at least one son if he carried on believing that this could happen. Hopefully, daughters too. He had to! If not for his own sake but mama's, and the duty he owed to his family name as the present Duke of Carlfield, to ensure its continuity.

Edward rubbed his eyes. He had been staring at the same set of figures for a while now and had lost concentration. The loss of Ruth, and the effect of this on his mother, had made him realise the importance of family. How no man was truly an island, and shouldn't try to live in isolation which he had been attempting to do for far too long. He was also well aware that if his father was still alive, he would more than likely have been encouraging him to produce an heir. Instead Edward had focused on, and taken pride in building his father's empire since he passed away. The time had gone quickly, and it was only recently that he realised he had been upholding the reputation and the family's name on his own for the last nine years.

This train of thought was interrupted by Jenkins, informing him that his mother wished if possible for him to have tea with her in the drawing room. Edward closed the ledger, and left the study to join her feeling surprised by the amount of small plates, covered in cakes and biscuits, which had been laid on the table for tea. Cynthia smiled as soon as she saw the look on his face, and told him that she wanted to create a relaxing atmosphere for when she conducted her interview with Miss Barlow.

Edward had mixed feelings about what she had done. It was a step too far too soon. It seemed that the Duchess had already decided Sophia would be a suitable replacement for Ruth so intended to befriend her, without even meeting her or taking part in an interview. Clearly this was wishful thinking, which was perfectly understandable and to some extent matched his own. He hoped very much that Owen's sister did impress his mother when the two ladies met. However it still concerned him that Ruth had set a high standard to follow. She truly had been a wonderful companion. Nothing had been too much trouble for her to do, and she seemed to understand the Duchess' every need. He sincerely hoped again that his mother wouldn't be disappointed with Miss Barlow in any way. For his own part he was prepared to dispense with the need for references since she was Owen's sister, a companion was needed very quickly, and he was happy to rely on his own judgement of character.

This train of thought was interrupted by Cynthia who told him that she wished he wouldn't travel as much, and reminded him once again of her wish for grandchildren. Especially now that she was older. What he had said last night at dinner gave her hope that he was going to take the matter more seriously. The Duchess hesitated at this point, but she clearly had something else she wished to say to him. So she continued by reminding Edward that she had hoped something more would come of his relationship with Felicity whom she now understood had given her husband, Lord Longford, a son.

The Duchess' words were enough to turn Owen's thoughts once again to his selfishness in waiting this long to find a spouse. Admittedly he had time on his side, since he wasn't yet thirty years of age, and however hard he tried he still wasn't entirely convinced that the right woman whom he could love would come along. Even when he did begin to look for her in earnest. Or at the very least believe he could make a life with. He began to frown, and quickly stopped himself. Not wishing his mother to see him doing it. Nevertheless she didn't know or understand why he had been quite so reticent in the past about speaking to Joey's father, and making a proposal for Felicity's hand in marriage.

Despite the imminent arrival of Mr and Miss Barlow, Ned knew that he couldn't wait any longer to tell his mother the real reason why he hadn't married. She had clearly only just found out that Felicity was now a mother. He went to stand next to her chair, and put his arm around her shoulders. "Mama, I am so sorry you feel hurt. I understand how much you want a daughter-in-law and grandchildren, and I also know how much you are troubled by Ruth leaving you so suddenly. However the loss of Felicity as a wife wasn't in any way due to laziness, or lack of attention on my part. It is difficult for me to tell you this, but in the same way as I loved Joey as a friend, I did have similar feelings for her. Nevertheless it wasn't quite so simple." Edward hesitated, and cleared his throat.

"After Joey was killed in a skirmish with Napoleon's soldiers before the Battle of Waterloo, it left an enormous hole in both of our hearts and lives. So that each time we looked at each other it reminded us too much of how close, and inseparable the three of us had been as children. Even so there was a part of me that still couldn't accept I wouldn't have been able to prevent my best friend's death. Even if I had been in France with him, which would have been against Papa's wishes for me to stay in England." Edward sighed heavily. "It was never really spoken of by Felicity and I, but I saw it in her eyes when they misted with tears after she looked into mine. Both of us had been badly hurt by Joey's death, and strangely enough because we had been so close when he was alive, we couldn't rely on this to console us. Every time we looked at each other we had too many memories. With the result that Felicity soon took to avoiding me whenever she could, and I couldn't pursue her. It didn't seem right or proper to do this. When the mourning period was finished and she came out, I understand that she accepted the first proposal she received. As you already know it was from Lord Longford, and now, Felicity has given him a son. I am very sorry I didn't feel able to tell you sooner, mama, about how I felt. However, my feelings for Felicity have begun to fade, and you have my word that I shall begin my search for a wife."

The way the Duchess of Carlfield said, "my poor boy, Ned, I am so very sorry. I didn't realise," only made him love her even more. Making the feeling stronger as she saw that her own eyes had filled with tears.

Neither of them had time to say anything else however, since Jenkins knocked politely on the door to announce the arrival of Miss Sophia Barlow for her interview.

Chapter 8

Sophia took a deep breath as she walked into the drawing room, and tried to calm her thudding heart. Wishing that Owen and Hannah had been able to accompany her, she suddenly noticed the most handsome gentleman she had ever seen looking at her. He stepped forward immediately to greet her, with a smile which reached his eyes. As if he sensed her discomfort, and wished very much to put her at ease. Edward introduced himself as the Duke of Carlfield before gesturing to an older woman whom he explained was his mother, Lady Cynthia Carlisle.

Sophia could feel the heat in her cheeks from the intensity of the Duke's gaze, and realised that she must be blushing. So much so that she had forgotten to curtsy. When she did remember it was almost too late so became rushed, and not as elegant as it ought to have been. However in that split second she knew, from the excitement and warmth she felt inside, that she had never been as attracted to anyone else in the same way as the Duke. Certainly not any of the gentlemen Lucas had arranged for her to meet. She also realised just how nice his mother looked. Cynthia was smiling at her kindly, and had motioned for her to take a seat. Whilst the housemaid who had appeared with a fresh pot of tea, since the first one had been left standing for too long without being poured, was attending to this. Having been instructed to do so by Jenkins, the Butler.

Sophia felt her hands tremble when she accepted the cup and saucer from her. Hoping that she wouldn't drop them, and disgrace herself. Thankfully she had politely refused to take the piece of the cake which had been also offered to her. The white icing on the top looked delicious, and her taste buds had responded accordingly, but the mere risk of speaking with her mouth full was enough to prevent this. Why did the Duke have to be quite so handsome, and a distraction she couldn't help thinking in frustration? When all she needed was to concentrate completely on the interview, to do her best. She had been drawn straight away into the intensity of his dark, brooding eyes. His broad shoulders and slim waist were equally attractive and although he wasn't fashionably dressed so far as she knew, but elegantly, it was definitely in the style of a gentleman. Without any outrageous colour for his cravat or waistcoat, which were both a subdued shade of blue. Almost the perfect match for her best dress, she couldn't help thinking but not understanding why this made her blush even more.

The interview was always going to be difficult, without the excitement she now felt because of being in such close proximity to him, and the deliciously warm feeling she had inside. While her inner voice was screaming at her that she must pull herself together, or risk not being able to present herself properly to her new employer, and face once again being doomed to a loveless marriage to Lord Dilley.

Meanwhile, Edward was watching Miss Barlow carefully. She was exceptionally nervous. Just then she looked up from her tea cup, and her hazel eyes met his. Edward was immediately mesmerised by the softness in them. She was equally moved by the light in his blue eyes, which fascinated her. At times it appeared almost green, and she was unable to avert her gaze. Resulting in them both staring at each other for a moment too long, which could easily have been deemed scandalous had they been in a different situation.

Much to his surprise Sophia's ethereal beauty had captivated the Duke, and this train of thought was soon interrupted by a delighted Cynthia. She hadn't failed to notice any of this, or that Sophia was exactly as she had hoped she would be. Very beautiful to the point of being willowy, softly spoken, and demure. Perfect for what she now had in mind. Moreover if she knew anything about it, which she did, nature had already started to play its part in the way Ned had looked at her. After his earlier admission about Joey's sister, Cynthia had soon felt the need to give her son a helping hand. She appreciated that some might well regard it as meddling, including himself. However she felt vindicated by the fact that she had become a lot more forgetful lately, which she hoped he hadn't noticed. She had begun to feel her increasing age, and this was the main reason she had wished to replace Ruth as quickly as possible. Even more so now, if the quite charming Miss

Sophia Barlow could also set Ned well and truly on the path to finding love.

There was also the niggling thought at the back of her mind that she was partially to blame for what had happened to Ned. Not that she had of course wanted him to die at Waterloo, but her husband wished initially to give his blessing to him accompanying Joey when he went to fight Napoleon. He said it was a matter of honour, and was proud that it was in his son's blood to do it. She was the one who had argued vehemently, and possibly selfishly, against it. Pointing out that Ned was his only heir, and May it never come to pass, what would happen if he didn't come back? Maybe she shouldn't have been quite as quick to think this. Given the effect which it ultimately had on Ned, but this was the opportunity now to make everything right again.

Having Sophia in their lives would give them both a new lease of life. Just because she wasn't like the rest of those mostly dreadful mamas she had to listen to every season, since she didn't have a daughter to launch, that didn't mean she couldn't help her only son find a wife. Albeit without letting him know what she was up to. She had always been a no nonsense sort of woman, which meant that she didn't have a great deal of hesitation now in giving Ned a helping hand when he needed it. He was obviously still grieving for the loss of Joey, and Felicity too.

Cynthia knew from her own experience of true love, that having the right woman share his life would cure him from the horror she anticipated he felt whenever he gazed sadly into the distance. If this occurred at the dining table his food would be left untouched, and he seemed so far away that he could no longer hear her voice speaking to him. Even though he was sitting in the most beautiful room beneath the most enchanting candlelight, being served exquisite food on the finest antique plates in the land, Ned was like a lost soul. Whilst it was her duty as his mother, especially now that his Papa was no longer with them, to help him make his way in life.

Cynthia had learned from her own marriage to his father, in particular at the end of his life, that it was only love which could save us in times of despair and hopelessness. A love which was so strong that it had the power to overcome whatever obstacles fate placed in our way, and make us truly want to live again. That was the love she wished for Ned, and made no apology for the way in which she was prepared now to help him get it. No, this was the right decision to make! Whatever polite society might think of his romance if it should be with Miss Sophia Barlow, and from the way they had looked at each other a moment ago, there was every chance it might well be. Cynthia sat up straight in her chair, even more determined than ever that this should work out well for them both, and her too.

As far as she was concerned, the other mamas could gossip as much as they wished to about the Duke marrying his servant, if it should happen that way, because they would still have had love in their lives. Something which sadly not everyone did. In reaching this decision the Duchess had however completely ignored the effect of being named in the scandal sheets, and being shunned by polite society. Since she believed what she read in them to be mostly wicked lies. There was far too much hypocrisy in the world now! She had also never been one for abiding by social rules set by others. People who caused great unhappiness, and should frankly know better.

She laughed then with delight at the possibility of her wish coming true, causing her to splutter into her tea, and Ned looked curiously at her. Not wishing to make him suspicious about what some might regard as a highly unladylike scheme, she turned it quickly into a cough. Using her embroidered handkerchief to cover her mouth. "All better now," she said, innocently enough, and with a beaming smile. Making him wonder what she had been thinking about. His heart sank when he imagined what it could have been, but at least she seemed to be in good spirits again for which he was grateful.

Still smiling Cynthia began the interview by asking Sophia to tell them a little about herself, and her education. Feeling that these were safe and easy subjects for her to talk about, without of course knowing the truth of the situation. That Sophia was already on the verge of causing a scandal by running away from home, and an arranged marriage to Lord Dilley.

Chapter 9

Without wishing to do so Sophia quickly looked away from the Duke, to smile at his mother instead. In her best softly spoken voice she politely expressed concern that her Ladyship had suffered the loss of Ruth, and how hard this must have been for her before she began to talk about the small, and relatively unknown, finishing school for young ladies which Lucas had found for her in Wales. Without adding that this had no doubt been a much cheaper option than sending her abroad or letting her stay in England. As anticipated neither the Duke nor Duchess had heard of it, but were happy for her to continue talking about what she had learned.

"Essentially I was taught to be a debutante, your Ladyship, and prepare for the London season which led to me being presented to Queen Charlotte. Unfortunately however, due to a pressing family matter, I was unable to continue the season this year. My brother advised me to seek employment with you, after he had spoken to the Duke," Sophia said, inclining her head respectfully to Edward, to acknowledge the part he had played in her being with them.

"I am very grateful that attending a finishing school also made me suitable as a ladies' companion. I have already been introduced to polite society, and learned the social skills I will need to satisfy your expectations. Of lesser importance I learned French for several months, perfected my dancing, and deportment, also how to curtsey properly with a level of dignity and poise."

Cynthia nodded in complete agreement with what Sophia had said, impressed by her presentation at Court, and asked her then about the accomplishments she was most proud of. That made Sophia's heart sink. Owen and her hadn't talked about the questions she might be asked, assuming that they would be straightforward and factual like the first one. Making her feel bewildered by the latest one. In her opinion her greatest achievement so far in life had to be writing poetry, and that she was a blue stocking, but she had already made her own mind up not to mention this.

Seeing her hesitation and alarm, the Duke attempted to help her reply to the question, by pointing out that there really was no need to be shy, which only made Sophia feel even more anxious than she already did. Since she regarded his observation as a likely criticism of her social skills. Realising she wouldn't have any longer to think about it or that there would be anything else she could truthfully say she began, hesitantly at first, to talk about her writing. Much to Cynthia's delight when Sophia's face came alive with joy, and a clear feeling of love for what she did. This also resulted in Edward not being able to stop himself from staring at her again. Miss Sophia Barlow was truly an extraordinary young lady, and had come into their lives like a breath of fresh air.

Nevertheless the Duke was feeling more than a little confused, which he couldn't solely attribute to the obvious attraction he felt for her. When she had walked through the door he had been stunned by how beautiful she was, clearly very intelligent, yet seemed to be attempting at first to present herself as one of those vapid debutantes he detested. She hadn't revealed the reason for her leaving the season. He hadn't however heard her name mentioned in connection with any of the current scurrilous gossip, but equally it didn't seem unreasonable to assume that a great beauty like her would have received any number of marriage proposals even though it was only her first season. He wondered why she hadn't simply accepted one of them, to prevent Owen's advice to her to seek employment. Although he didn't agree with marrying where love wasn't at the heart of it, that was by far the easiest way out for so many young women who didn't otherwise have the means to support themselves.

He also assumed correctly that there was a definite spark to her personality beneath the subdued exterior she had projected, which only served to intrigue him. There was clearly a lot more to Miss Sophia Barlow than met the eye. The question now was whether he could take the chance of employing her when she didn't have any previous experience of being a ladies' companion, or what this actually entailed. Even more importantly there was something which he couldn't quite put his finger on, and that she wasn't telling them about her personal circumstances.

It was clear that his mother liked her enormously, and wished him to appoint her. Judging by the encouraging looks she had been giving him. Along with the occasional tap on his ankle with her shoe, which had grown harder the longer the interview continued. Nevertheless it had to be said that the Duchess did have an impetuous nature, and he had inherited the duty from his father of having to manage this from time to time, to avoid her getting into difficulty. However, knowing from experience that she also liked to get her own way and could be quite difficult when she didn't, maybe he should give Sophia the benefit of the doubt despite his reservations? He had been intending to do this earlier, since he had met her father and liked her brother enormously. There was also the matter of her being the only applicant for the position.

Even though he wouldn't be there to oversee her employment Mrs Agnes Pender, the housekeeper in Yorkshire, was highly trusted by him along with of course Jenkins. They could deal with any impropriety which might occur during his absence abroad, if an intervention proved necessary, which he of course hoped it wouldn't. All this was less than ideal, but it could be the only solution to the dilemma. He really didn't want to lose the trading agreement with Lord Watson by not going to Paris, or incur the Duchess' wrath by not employing who she wished as a companion. Mostly however, irrespective of her employment, he needed to distance himself from the infatuation he felt for Miss Barlow when this was highly inappropriate.

Meanwhile the two ladies were deeply engrossed in conversation about the poetry they liked to read. Sophia discovered that Lady Cynthia enjoyed a wide variety of verse, and novels. Including her favourite William Butler Yeats, and much to her delight, Miss Jane Austen. She was able to respond by telling her ladyship that she was still reading Northanger Abbey. The Duchess also apparently liked being read to, and said that she found Sophia's voice gentle and soothing, which Edward also couldn't deny.

Until Sophia became so carried away by the conversation and sheer joy that her employer wouldn't prevent her from reading as much as she wished to, the truth came out then that she also loved writing her own verse. Cynthia was very impressed by this, and began to talk about the soiree she had already arranged when there would be poetry readings. Both of them became very excited by the prospect of this, and the Duke was delighted to see his mother become so animated. Ruth hadn't unfortunately been as well educated as Sophia, or a great reader. Despite the Duchess trying to encourage her to pick up a book at every opportunity, and although she tried her best, she obviously wasn't a great lover of reading but more well versed in the practicalities of being a ladies' companion.

Sophia's heart was racing, and she summoned all of the willpower she possibly could to appear composed. When she caught the Duke staring at her again with his dark, and brooding, eyes this had felt a little intimidating. Despite her attraction to him, he was a titled gentleman whereas she was a merchant's daughter, far below him on the social scale and even worse than that, not being entirely honest about her circumstances. Nevertheless she hadn't experienced anything in the past like her feelings for him now. She could sense the power within him, and his strength, which made the butterflies in her stomach begin to flutter. She couldn't understand why Owen hadn't warned her that the Duke could be so intimidating. Especially when he started to frown, as he did now. Giving her reason to tear her eyes away from him.

Sophia decided then that there would be little or no advantage in exaggerating her own accomplishments. Why would the Duke of Carlfield and his mother be interested in that? A tiny voice inside reminded her that she was already being less than honest with them, so she should at least tell the truth about everything else. Then again, if she proved herself to be an excellent companion as she fully intended to try to do, would it really matter to them later why she had wanted the position? Surely a powerful duke and his mother wouldn't be interested in her personal life? Why should they be? Sophia began to feel a little better once she had thought of this, and began to tell Cynthia about the nature poem she was still working on.

Sophia was completely caught off guard when the Duchess became incapable of containing her excitement, and said that she would like to appoint her as a companion. Much to the surprise of the Duke who had rather assumed that the decision would be his to make. Although he would of course have consulted the Duchess first. Nevertheless, irrespective of all the reasons he had already told himself should be against it, he was inclined to agree with her when they discussed it later that Miss Barlow seemed to be the perfect choice.

He took control of the conversation at that point, to remind Sophia and his mother of his intention for them to leave London the folowing morning, and travel by carriage to Yorkshire. So the offer which had been made was subject to Miss Barlow being able to travel with them,to which Sophia readily agreed.

Hannah was waiting inside her carriage, whilst Owen walked up and down outside, since they were without a chaperone. It was a bittersweet moment when Sophia told them her news. They were highly delighted on the one hand that she would be able to escape marrying Lord Dilley, but not that this also meant they would no longer see each other for some time if all went well for Sophia in her new position, as they very much hoped it would. Hannah said immediately that her carriage would call for her in the morning, to take her back to Belgravia, so that she wouldn't be late to travel to the Duke's Yorkshire estate.

Later that evening, Sophia was busy packing her belongings putting the pearl and coral necklace carefully into the smaller bag she intended to keep with her at all times. Along with a handkerchief, and the small amount of money Owen had been able to give her. Assuring her that he could easily manage to do this when she expressed concern. Not wishing her to leave without any money at all, he told her that she must spend it if she wanted, or needed to. Although he was certain that her new employer would take care of any emergency which might arise. The Duke of Carlfield was an honourable gentleman, so she need not be afraid of being part of his household.

Owen had also told her that he had spoken briefly to Edward after she had joined Hannah in the carriage, and the Duke confirmed that she had made an excellent impression on the Duchess. However, he didn't of course admit to the effect which Sophia had on him, so Owen remained unaware of this. He did however add that he would make certain she was well cared for while she was under his roof, the same as he did for all of his servants, helping to dismiss Owen's fears for Sophia. All he had to do now was make sure that she left safely, and Lucas didn't discover her whereabouts.

Thankfully he had also been able to confirm that Lucas would be out all evening. Furthermore. as he was expecting to drink a lot of alcohol which he often did, he would stay the night at one of his favourite clubs and wouldn't be home until late the following morning. Fate had once again been in Sophia's favour! This meant that she would have sufficient time to make her escape while he wasn't at home. Hopefully even be well on the way out of London, before he became aware of her absence.

Meanwhile Edward was seated at the dinner table with his mother while the servants were getting ready to move back to Yorkshire the following day. Most of them were thrilled by the prospect of it, regarding the north of England as their home. Despite the hustle and bustle of London being a welcome change every year the general opinion remained that it was always nice to go home, and see the loved ones they had left behind.

The Duke's thoughts were however filled with Sophia. He hadn't expected her to be as beautiful as she was, and had to continually remind himself that she was far beyond his reach as his mother's companion. There couldn't possibly be anything romantic between them. Irrespective of how much he desired this. He could imagine the scandal it would cause if a prominent duke of the land, such as himself, was to begin courting a lady so far beneath his social rank. He could still see the indignation on the faces of those persistent mama's in London, who couldn't believe he wasn't interested in any of their daughters, which almost made him smile again. Whilst Miss Sophia Barlow was entirely different to them. His mother also couldn't stop herself from repeatedly commenting on what a lovely young woman she was. Leaving Edward to summon every ounce of willpower he had, so as to not seem too interested in her, and encourage the Duchess in any of the plotting she might have in mind.

He was more than ever now secretly relieved to be going abroad. It would give him good reason to stay away from the fantasising he felt certain his mother was doing, about the enchanting Miss Barlow and himself. Ned knew her well enough to realise that a possible romance, between her new companion and son, could easily have become her latest scheme to create a better world. However inappropriate this might be the Duchess was often perfectly content to ignore social convention, leaving it to him to guide her. Irrespective of how difficult it might prove to be on this occasion.

Chapter 10

The following morning Sophia was woken at dawn by Amy knocking quietly on the door of her bedchamber. The maid was holding a tray with a cup of tea on it which she had made for her. Amy was always the first one to get up in the morning. One of her duties was to get everything ready for the family before they left their beds. Including lighting the fires in winter, and boiling water for them to wash. So not long afterwards she returned with a jug of hot water.

Although she hadn't intended to at first, Sophia had told her about her plan to leave that morning after swearing the maid to secrecy on the small silver locket she always wore under her dress. Sophia knew this had been a gift from her mother before she left home to go into service. Also that she treasured it dearly, since it had been in their family for many years. So both of them appreciated the gravity of the promise she made not to reveal Sophia's secret, and that she would not only be letting herself down but also her mother and family if she did.

When Amy said that she wasn't in the least surprised by her decision to go, she had hoped that Sophia would reveal her intended destination, but all she would say was that she had found a safe place. The two young women hugged each other realising just how much they would miss each other's companionship. "Promise me that if things get any worse here, Amy, you will find another position," Sophia said, anxiously. Afraid that she would be the next one to fall foul of Lucas' bad temper.

"I promise, but it won't be the same here without you, Miss Sophia. I shall do my best to also be gone before too long, but I need to have another position to move to before I can leave. So that I can carry on sending the little I earn back to my mama. My family would suffer if I didn't, so I will carry on here for the time being," Amy said, with tears in her eyes.

Sophia hugged her again, and told her to keep herself safe. She hoped they would meet again one day. Amy gave Sophia her mother's address then, if she ever needed another place to go. She told her that it wasn't much, but she knew her brothers would soon send Lucas on his way if he turned up there. However unlikely it might be that he would think of looking for his sister inside the warren of streets behind Whitechapel Road in London's East End! Amy had smiled then, and wished Sophia well.

Not having very much of her own from which she could choose a gift, she asked Amy if she would like to keep the dress with the pink flowers embroidered on it, since they were a similar size. After some discussion as to why she didn't think she should take it, the dress was duly handed over to her by an insistent Sophia. On the understanding that she would hide it for now, and take it to her mother's house the following afternoon when she had her one free afternoon in the month.

Amy was thrilled with the present. She had always loved, and admired the dress whenever she laid it on the bed for Sophia to put on for a social engagement. Never dreaming that she would own anything like it herself. Even though she had heard that in some of the more well-to-do households ladies did pass on their unwanted clothes to the servants. However, she knew how little Sophia had for herself so was still reluctant to take it. Until Sophia became creative with the truth, and told her that she would have plenty of new clothes where she was going. Without actually knowing this, but hoping it might be true.

Amy stroked the embroidery gently, before saying again how beautiful the dress was. Then several times how grateful she was to receive such an expensive gift, and thanked Sophia profusely for giving it to her before rolling the dress carefully into a bundle, and wrapping it in a towel Sophia had decided to leave behind. Leaving Amy to wonder later where exactly she was going, as she concocted all sorts of amazing adventures for her in her own imagination.

However once everything was ready and Sophia was definitely leaving, the stark reality of the situation left both of them with serious faces. Amy had also brought Sophia some bread and butter, with a slice of meat, she had taken from the pantry. Not caring what Cook would say when she noticed it was gone. Giving the food to Sophia to eat on her journey, as she would be leaving without any breakfast. Sophia had smiled sadly, and put the small package in the small bag where she had packed her mother's necklaces. There were only two other bags containing her belongings. As soon as she was ready to leave Amy took these down the back stairs, and through the kitchen to the rear door of the house, closely followed by Sophia. The young women hurried when they heard Cook moving about inside her room. Neither of them wished to receive any curious stares or questions about where Miss Sophia was going.

Fortunately they reached the door without meeting anyone else. Amy took the large key from the hook on the wall, and unlocked it before passing the bags to Sophia. With one last hug which was over almost as soon as it began, she disappeared into the London fog. Amy watched for a moment, but since she couldn't see her any more she closed the door quickly in case anyone else came into the passageway behind her, and asked what she was doing.

Sophia hurried across the backyard to the gate in the wall, and pulled the bolt across to open it. Wishing that it hadn't made such a loud noise, she decided not to waste any time looking behind her. Even though it was almost light the fog had hidden everything in the distance. Fortunately she could at least see far enough ahead to walk a few steps at a time. She could also hear people out and about on the street ahead. Making her afraid that there might be vagrants or scoundrels hiding in wait for her. By the time she was hurrying along the street Sophia's heart was beating very loudly. She became afraid then that Lucas might return home unexpectedly, and catch her. However in what was actually only a few minutes, she reached Hannah's carriage without mishap. Giving her bags to the coachman who had been waiting for her, she quickly climbed inside, and he closed the door behind her. Never so glad to see anyone in her life before, as she did Hannah.

During the carriage ride to the Duke of Carlfield's house, she made Sophia promise to write to her as soon as she had settled into her new home. Making Sophia cry again. In that moment, the reality of the situation had become even clearer to her. For the first time in her life, she was going to be separated from her best friend, and all she had ever known. The two young women became frightened then of the unknown, and spent the rest of the journey holding onto each other for comfort. Neither of them knew what they would do without the other. Remembering how they had plotted and planned to outwit Lucas in the past; get the books Sophia wanted to read, without him knowing anything about it; their endless conversations about falling in love, and the trips out in Hannah's carriage when they had so much fun. All of that would no longer happen, and they realised for the first time how large a gap this would create in their lives.

On the way to Belgravia the carriage came to a halt at the entrance of Hyde Park and Sophia looked out of the window, trying desperately to see Owen through the fog. She couldn't see him because he had been waiting further away and had dismounted as soon as he noticed their arrival. A highly emotional Sophia flung her arms around him when he opened the carriage door telling him that she would miss him terribly. She hadn't been parted from him except when she attended the finishing school, but had always known when she would be coming back, and she thanked him again from the bottom of her heart for helping her.

"I wish that I could have done more, Sophia. You deserve so much more than having to work as a lady's companion. I will hope every single day that you remain safe and well, that good fortune follows you, and you soon find the gentleman you have always dreamed of who will love and care for you as it should be done," Owen said, kissing her forehead, gently.

Sophia was overcome with emotion when he added that she reminded him so much of their mother who would have been very proud of the woman she had become. "You must go now, sister. It wouldn't do to keep the Duke, and Duchess waiting. Since you won't be able to write to me directly in case Lucas finds the letters, Hannah will keep me updated on your progress when you write to her."

When Sophia took Owen's hand and squeezed it, she saw him exchange a look with Hannah, which revealed again how much sadness they felt at her departure. He squeezed her hand gently, before releasing it to close the door. While Hannah and her watched him get back onto his horse, they waved from the carriage window and Sophia hoped that he had seen them through the fog.

A short while later, the carriage came to a halt outside the Duke of Carlfield's house. In another tearful goodbye Sophia hugged Hannah tightly until the coachman coughed discreetly, since one of Edward's footmen was waiting to help her alight from the carriage.

It was all Sophia could do to summon enough willpower not to burst into tears as she stood on the path next to her bags, and watched Hannah's carriage leaving her behind.

Chapter 11

As soon as Edward had finished his breakfast, he went to speak to Jenkins to check that the carriage was ready to leave since he was eager to start the journey. It would take them three days to reach Carlfield House, his country seat, and he was expecting to find it as tedious as usual. With innumerable stops to change the horses, and at other times, overnight or for lunch at a coaching inn. Nevertheless his carriage was more comfortable than most, with the family coat of arms on the doors. Although this did make it a possible target for highwaymen, and the reason why the servants' carriages also travelled with them.

The coachman was also a man who reputedly had the strength of an ox which the Duke didn't doubt, and one of the grooms whom he knew wasn't averse to using his knuckles in a fight, sat on the seat at the back watching their progress from behind. However Edward still felt uncomfortable about the safety of the Duchess and his servants when travelling with them, and he wished to get the whole thing over and done with as quickly as possible. Also because he would need to ride to the coast shortly afterwards, to board a ship which would take him across the Channel to France, then travel on horseback again through the regions to Paris.

He groaned inwardly. Not always being the most patient of men, but which he always tried to hide especially from the Duchess. They would be able to leave London as soon as she had completed her travel preparations, and Miss Barlow had arrived, which hopefully wouldn't be too long. So his heart missed a beat when he noticed that she was already standing quietly by herself in the hallway. Alerted to her arrival by the footman, Jenkins had invited her into the house where he said she would be able to wait more comfortably, and said that her bags would be taken to the carriage.

Sophia immediately dipped a curtsy in greeting the Duke who couldn't help feeling captivated all over again by her presence. Although he noted with concern that she seemed to have been crying, and certainly wasn't quite as composed as she ought to have been. Then he reminded himself for the umpteenth time that Miss Sophia Barlow was his employee, and that it was very wrong for him to have any feelings of attraction for her. As a result he felt greatly relieved when the Duchess began walking down the stairs towards them.

Cynthia was smiling profusely when she said good morning to Edward. She was also clearly delighted to see Sophia, and greeted her warmly. The two women exchanged a few pleasantries until they heard Jenkins informing the Duke that the carriage was ready, if his Lordship and the ladies wished to step outside. Edward turned to his mother to seek her permission, and with a satisfied nod at him, she indicated to Sophia that she should take her arm along with the small bag she was holding which she duly did.

As they were leaving the house, Edward overheard Cynthia informing Sophia that she would be riding with them. This came as a complete surprise to him, since for some reason he had been under the impression she would be travelling with the rest of the servants. However, it wasn't long before he recalled that Ruth often used to travel with them, and he didn't know why he had thought it would be different for Sophia. Especially since Mama might well need her help during the journey, and was likely to want to talk to her to pass the time. Whilst Edward would have much preferred it if she had travelled with the other servants. Her presence was simply too disturbing, and for his own comfort he wished to keep as much distance from her as possible. However, good manners wouldn't allow him to object to his mother's wishes which weren't unreasonable.

Without thinking about what he was doing the Duke helped his mother get into the carriage, before he realised that politeness would demand that he also extend his hand to Sophia in the same way. An intense awareness of her proximity coursed through his body as she moved closer to him, to place her hand trustingly inside his own. He knew that he ought not feel the desire for her so deeply within himself, but couldn't help it. Even more so when she had withdrawn her hand from his, to take the seat alongside his mama, and he felt the loss of her. Their eyes had met only briefly in a single intoxicating moment, before that was over too. The Duke's heart sank when he knew it wasn't to be repeated.

He quickly took the seat opposite the Duchess, feeling highly disgruntled and ill at ease. Until she asked him politely, in his opinion with a far from innocent look in her eyes, if he wouldn't mind moving to sit opposite Sophia. As she needed more room to stretch her legs on the journey, to avoid the horror of suffering from cramp which she was certain Ned wouldn't willingly wish to inflict on her. He was of course obliged to do so, and if that wasn't bad enough, the Duchess insisted then that he should desist from calling her companion Miss Barlow. At least when there was no one else present. Sophia was a delightful name, and she wished to hear him use it. Placing Edward once again in a difficult position.

However the Duke of Carlfield was obliged to do as his mother had asked, since it was a simple enough request. Despite Sophia blushing profusely at the familiarity of it, and both of them feeling more than a little overwhelmed by Cynthia's interference. At least she didn't give Sophia permission to call him Edward he thought, and which she had actually deemed to be a step too far, but did go on to ask Sophia to refer to her as Lady Cynthia in the future. Since she would feel much more comfortable with this.

Quite satisfied with how much progress had already been made, Lady Cynthia went on to chatter non-stop about inconsequential things, feeling perfectly at ease. Ignoring the obvious discomfort of her son and companion, whom she was certain would become accustomed to each other in time and her meddling.

As Cynthia's voice continued in the background and the carriage jolted uncomfortably over the ruts in the road on their way out of London, followed by the servants' carriages, neither of them knew what to do with their legs to avoid getting too close to the other. Especially when they were almost thrown from their seats by the poor condition of the road. Nevertheless, determined to maintain a sense of social propriety Edward and Sophia tried their best not to look directly at each other, despite being fully aware of their proximity. Trying at first to busy themselves in their own pursuits, and ignore it.

Sophia listened politely to Lady Cynthia, and replied to her questions about the places they were passing. Whilst Edward soon felt tired of his newspaper, and of how difficult he found it trying to pretend he wasn't in such an awkward predicament. Wishing with all of his heart to take the most beautiful woman he had ever seen into his arms, and kiss her. Something which he obviously couldn't do since this behaviour would be too shocking for words. At the same time the incessant rocking of the carriage made it almost impossible for his leg not to collide with hers, from time to time.

On one occasion he felt his eyes soften, without him intending it to happen, and she also apparently hadn't been able to stop herself from mirroring his look. As if she knew and understood his thoughts, which she shared. However she had still wrenched her eyes away from him again, before very long.

The Duchess was also by now telling her in great detail about the Carlisle family, and their ancestors, which again made the Duke uncomfortable. Eventually including some of her own reminiscences of his childhood, much to his great displeasure. Feeling that like the tea party atmosphere she had tried to create yesterday at Sophia's interview, all of this was a step too soon, and most likely too far. When he tried to object to her recounting certain events which she had found charming, she attributed his embarrassment to false modesty, and chuckled. She did however stop for a time to gaze out of the window, and talk about what she recalled of the places in London she had visited across the years. Meanwhile Sophia had been intrigued by all of it.

Although Edward slept well the night before, and had only just left his bed, he decided that the safest option for him would be to feign sleep. The less interaction he had with Miss Sophia Barlow, and his mother's chattering, the better. He couldn't help feeling relieved that he would soon be away from all of this for several weeks, and if this morning was the measure of it, his mother would manage quite well without him. Now that she had Sophia, as her new companion.

So after making his excuses to the Duchess, Ned closed his eyes. A part of him was sorry that he couldn't also block out their voices. In particular, Sophia's, which was soft and gentle. Just like her, he couldn't help thinking.

Chapter 12

It wasn't until the Duke's carriage had been on the road for several hours that Sophia began to feel more at ease. Cynthia had done her best to lighten the atmosphere. Drawing her into conversation about a variety of topics which she clearly thought would interest her and making her stop being quite so afraid of making a mistake. Or even worse, losing her new position after it had only just begun. It seemed too that Lady Cynthia was more than happy to provide instructions on how to perform her duties as a ladies' companion, if she didn't know what to do.

Moreover the further away from London they went in the Carlisle family carriage the safer Sophia felt. Gazing out of the window at the incredible sights she hadn't often seen, if at all. From the cows and sheep grazing in the fields to the orchards they passed, and Inns where they broke their journey, providing a welcome relief for both Lady Cynthia and her from the jarring movement of the carriage. When they alighted this gave her the opportunity to look at Ned, without him noticing her doing it. Her eyes secretly followed him as he was overseeing everything, talking to the coachman and other servants. She noticed him changing the grooms, to allow them to rest before travelling at the back of the carriages for too long, which she knew was an act of kindness.

After a while she also came to realise how much the Duchess shared her love of poetry and books, also somewhat to her surprise, the gardens and parks in London. She recounted the details of many happy hours spent visiting them with Ruth, before she told Sophia about her son's extensive grounds at his country seat which she was looking forward to sharing with her. She said that there was a lake, dovecote, the orange house where the head gardener grew a pineapple or two, and of course the rose garden. The Duchess clearly loved all of it, and both of them soon became quite excited by the thought of the many walks they could take around the grounds. Her Ladyship also appeared to know the names of the multitude of plants and flowers growing there. Sophia listened to her talking about them whilst trying her best not to mention her own situation, in case Lady Carlfield had heard of Lucas and his misdeeds.

There was only one occasion when she felt that she had said far too much, and tried to remain silent after that. Feeling invigorated by Lady Cynthia's description of the London gardens she loved, Sophia had spoken about her passion for Vauxhall Gardens, and the times she had been there with Hannah and her family. The Duchess had listened politely to her description of the lights, and so on before asking for the name of Hannah's parents. She was delighted that her companion was at last on the point of being more open with her, but Sophia realised her mistake immediately after the Duchess' question. Since it was inevitable that the Duchess of Carlfield would know Lord and Lady Audley, Hannah's parents, she couldn't reveal their identity, again for fear of word getting back to Lucas about her whereabouts, she began to cough into her handkerchief so dramatically that all thought of their names were gone by the time she had finished.

Except for Edward who had his eyes closed while he listened to them talking, delighted that all was well. Nevertheless Sophia's coughing fit had seemed contrived to say the least, and he began to wonder about her reasons for doing it. She surely wasn't hiding something from his mother by not telling her what she had asked? If so, that was something he wouldn't be able to accept, irrespective of how delightful she was otherwise. Once again the Duke had the feeling that Miss Barlow might not be everything she appeared to be. Although he didn't intend to alert the Duchess to his suspicions for the time being, since he didn't have any actual proof of her wrongdoing, he felt compelled to keep an eye on the situation. Nevertheless, he would have to instruct Jenkins to maintain a discreet and watchful eye during his absence abroad and so would Mrs Pender, the housekeeper. Quite diplomatically put to them of course, as it would never do to have the servants under the impression that he condoned them spying on each other. No! It had to be done discreetly, which he was certain Jenkins and Mrs Agnes Pender would manage admirably.

Meanwhile Cynthia was most displeased with Ned for pretending to be asleep when she knew for certain that he wasn't. She had seen the corners of his mouth twitch on several occasions, if she wasn't mistaken and rarely was. Looking as if he wished to laugh, but knew he couldn't because of his ruse. She wished that he had instead behaved like the charming man she knew he was, beneath that dreadful brooding exterior he adopted after Joey's death. Although her heart softened again when she recalled what he had told her privately about the subsequent loss of Felicity.

She sighed inwardly. It would take time she supposed for him to recover fully, knowing how much she still missed Ned's father, and such a pity that he would be travelling abroad so soon after he had seen Sophia and her safely installed at the house. During one of the brief pauses in the conversation she had scrutinised her new companion, taking in every detail of her face and appearance. Sophia had looked a little bedraggled earlier, but she had put this down to their early start. Nothing that the maid she had in mind to give her wouldn't be able quite easily to remedy.

Sophia had likewise been forming a better impression of the Duchess whom she thought was refined and elegant, but more importantly in her opinion kind, extremely well read and knowledgeable. She seemed to enjoy talking to all manner of people in society, and as a result, knew a lot about life. It was going to be a fascinating experience spending so much time with her, she couldn't help thinking. Realising again with an aching heart that this might well have been the sort of relationship she could have had with her own mother had she lived.

They had spoken again about their favourite poets. Before Cynthia had asked her about the verse she wrote and Sophia found herself able to talk about it. Even the frustration she felt as a writer in not being able to finish a poem when she was called away to do something else. Quickly realising her mistake, and that her time still wouldn't be her own at Carlfield, she blushed and begged the Duchess' forgiveness which touched the older woman's heart. So much so that Cynthia told Sophia, quite categorically, that she must stop saying how sorry she was. Both Ned and her wanted her to be very happy, living with them. Whilst the Duchess would ensure that she had more than enough time to finish all of her poems, but on one condition. Sophia had paled then not daring to imagine what it might be. However it was only that she should share her words with her, since she was very keen to hear them.

Meanwhile Sophia was beginning to find the Duke a little intimidating. Sitting opposite them asleep, which she had thought until then people only did in the privacy of their bedchambers. However, as always, it might be easier if only he wasn't quite so handsome! Irrespective of how many times her imagination might explore the possibility of a romance he was still her employer, and according to the social rules he followed, she could only ever be his servant.

Even more importantly she also couldn't take the risk of Lucas finding her, and forcing her marriage to Lord Dilley to go ahead. She needed to concentrate on that. The silly mistake she had made in mentioning Hannah by name definitely couldn't happen again. She was far safer simply staying as she was, a humble lady's companion, without having any illusions of grandeur concerning a romance with the Duke of Carlfield. Not forgetting of course the impropriety of such a situation, and disgrace, should it be discovered.

Sophia shuddered then. Imagining that she could feel Lucas and Lord Dilley reaching out to her from a distance. They would both know by now that she had gone, and Lucas would be furiously questioning everyone about her whereabouts. Any suffering they had to endure because of it was all her fault. How much she wished now that wasn't the case. A stray tear escaped from her eye, and she brushed it away quickly before anyone else should see.

Nevertheless it didn't escape the Duchess' notice, who put it down to Sophia being homesick. Wishing immediately to put a stop to this she asked her if she was getting cold. Before Sophia could reply, she passed her the extra shawl she had brought, which was lying idle on the seat next to her. As it was a warm day, Sophia thanked her very much and tried to refuse such a kind offer, saying that she was fine. Cynthia though insisted that she make use of it. The shawl was only light, and she wouldn't have Sophia feeling the cold draught from the window.

Sophia was taken aback by her kindness, and put the shawl around her shoulders straight away. Strangely enough, having it there did feel comforting and it wasn't too warm. Owen had always cared for her as well as he could, but Sophia hadn't received small gestures like this while she was growing up, and it reminded her again of how much she had missed because of not having a mother for most of her life. She couldn't help wondering then what her life would have been like if her mother had still been alive. She certainly wouldn't have been in the Duke of Carlfield's carriage in a compromising situation.

This train of thought was interrupted by the carriage coming to a halt, so that the horses could be changed again. Sophia glanced at the Duke who had opened his eyes, seemingly startled by being woken suddenly, and quickly averted them from looking at her face. Quickly she turned to Lady Cynthia who was smiling to herself, and already making preparations to alight. The journey progressed in much the same way, with innumerable stops when they left the carriage and returned to it. Until everything became a blur to Sophia, with her senses bombarded by new experiences, so much so that she stopped counting the times they alighted.

Meanwhile Edward continued to have reservations about what was now happening directly in front of him. Apart from how he felt personally about the proximity of Miss Barlow, he remained concerned that his mother was in the process of making too much of their relationship too soon. Sophia wasn't Ruth, and the appointment might not work out. He still wasn't sure what it was, but he couldn't help feeling instinctively that she was hiding something. Even if he was wrong, and he wasn't usually about someone else's character, it still took a lot more than just a few hours to get to know that person properly.

As a result he took Cynthia to one side when they stopped on the second evening, and insisted that Sophia eat with the servants. To which his mother immediately objected, as he expected her to. When Edward told her quite clearly that he wouldn't have it, she relented, and decided not to press the point. Not wishing to antagonise him, also fully appreciating the need to wheedle sometimes to get what she wanted. However, it was a shame. Sophia was a lovely, young woman. Exactly what Ned needed, if only he could see it!

Nevertheless she was prepared to concede that maybe he was right up to a point, in suggesting that this would be a good opportunity for Sophia to get to know some of the other servants in his household, before she met those who had stayed at Carlfield. As a result Cynthia asked her maid, Florence, to look after her companion for a short time. Telling Sophia that Ned and her had a private matter to discuss over dinner, so she wouldn't be required.

Sophia was a little alarmed by this at first, but soon took to Florence's warm manner and friendliness which reminded her of Amy. There were refreshments in the carriage, which the Duchess had instructed her to serve not long after they had set off from the London house, telling Ned and her that she hadn't had the inclination to eat her own breakfast earlier, due to being too excited about returning to Yorkshire. Sophia had intended to try to eat Amy's bread and meat when they stopped, as she was feeling very hungry by this time, but which hadn't in the end proved necessary.

She devoted her attention instead to scribbling notes in her journal which she kept on her lap, and intended later to turn into verse. Reluctant to lose any of the new experiences, or her thoughts about them and knowing that she wouldn't be able to remember everything if she didn't do this. What she didn't realise was how impressed Lady Cynthia was by her dedication, and taking the opportunity to learn everything she could about a world with which she wasn't yet familiar. Sophia's passion was reflected in her eyes when she wrote, and Cynthia had been particularly annoyed with Ned since he was once again pretending to be asleep so had missed it. What a foolish young man he was at times, she couldn't help thinking in frustration! Sighing inwardly, after realising it was precisely why he needed her help in matters of the heart.

Meanwhile Sophia was describing her impressions of the last inn they had visited. The animation in her voice made her face appear even more beautiful, and Cynthia felt that she truly was a breath of fresh air in their lives.

Chapter 13

Sophia had been imagining all sorts of things about the Carlfield estate from the Duchess' descriptions of it, the history of the house itself and family, along with vast acres of land all of it occupied. Her thoughts had wandered back to Northanger Abbey and the gothic romance stories she had read, as the carriage travelled along the country lanes of Yorkshire when the sun was setting. Nothing had however prepared her for just how stunning her first sight of it was from the carriage window. After Lady Cynthia had invited her to look, she had immediately put her hand across her mouth, with wonder and surprise. The lake in front of it was surrounded by reeds, swaying gently in the warm breeze, as the mellow stones of the sprawling property and its lawns basked in the late sunlight.

Lady Cynthia had told her during the journey from London that it had been rebuilt in the sixteen hundreds after the manor house from two hundred years earlier, possibly more, had burned to the ground. Whilst the present house was much larger than Sophia had imagined it, and again as Lady Cynthia had told her, with stables and outbuildings at the rear. The closer the carriage came to the property, enabled Sophia to see a part of the gardens which Cynthia had described, leaving her speechless, and unable to help thinking that it was the most wonderful house she had ever seen.

As soon as the coachman slowed the horses down to turn into the grounds, Edward looked quickly out of the window to check exactly where they were, and began to get to his feet. Eager to climb out of the confines of the carriage. He was helping his mother alight when he noticed that the same footman who brought Sophia to Jenkins' notice, when she had arrived at his house in Belgravia, was assisting her again. This time to alight from the other door. Causing the Duke to feel an intense surge of jealousy flow through him. Made worse by the great care which the footman was taking while standing far too close to her for the sake of decency, in his Lordship's opinion. There was also the matter of the disrespectful way he had of smiling up at her. As far as the Duke was concerned his mother's companion was a single woman under his protection, but which didn't give him the right to interfere with any other man in whom she might have an interest. Other than if this should of course affect the way she performed her duties. Or to reprimand the young footman who wasn't presumably going about the duties which would have been assigned to him by Jenkins.

Despite his annoyance Edward certainly didn't have any wish to appear churlish in front of Sophia. Also no doubt cause his mother to comment on his bad mood, if he put a stop to this now. These thoughts soon became tangled in his own longing to help Sophia down, and take her arm. Until he could no longer think straight or avert his eyes from what was happening in front of him.

He was eventually interrupted by Cynthia, asking him if he felt unwell. When all he could do was shake his head quickly, and miserably, in response. Knowing that he would probably not be able to make an excuse, without his voice sounding irritated and far too brusque, which would make her ask him even more questions that he didn't feel able to deal with. Anger, and intense frustration had by then replaced his initial jealousy.

Obviously the sooner he was away from the temptations of Miss Sophia Barlow the better, he thought as he took the Duchess' arm. Intending to greet the housekeeper and other servants who had been left in Yorkshire, and were now lined up on the circular path where the carriages stopped, before he accompanied his mother into the house.

Meanwhile the footman, Jimmy Wilson, had left Sophia to her own devices. With her smile and delightful voice thanking him, as he turned away from her, since he did have duties to attend to. She had noticed Florence behind Cynthia, so went to stand next to her. To wait with the other London servants, and follow them inside through the rear entrance, if the Duchess didn't need her once she had gone inside with the Duke. The ladies' maid whispered to her that this had been a family tradition for many years. Dating back to before her time and the late Duke of Carlfield, the present Duke's father, who had decided that their return from the London season should in the future be done like this.

As soon as Edward and his mother had gone through the great door into the hall, Jenkins passed a sealed letter to him which was marked urgent. Meanwhile the Duchess who had wanted Sophia to stay with her was introducing her new companion to the housekeeper, Mrs Agnes Pender. The Duke glanced at them. Delighted to see that Sophia was back where she belonged at the Duchess' side, and wouldn't come to any harm there. Immediately he informed Cynthia that he regretfully had a business matter he needed to attend to in his study.

A few moments later Edward was seated in the leather armchair behind a very large desk, similar to the one he had in London, reading the contents of the letter he had received. The frown had returned to his face. It was from Lord Watson who wished to inform him that his sister had fallen ill, and he had been obliged to go to her. For that reason he had no choice other than to postpone their business transaction in Paris.

Edward groaned. This meant that he would have to stay at Carlfield House. Conversely he was also well aware that his mother would be very happy to hear that he wasn't going away after all. All the trouble he had gone to in finding her a new companion so quickly had been unnecessary! Nevertheless the Duke didn't feel as disappointed as he believed he should be, and realised then that he was secretly relieved. Giving him time to make doubly sure that his mother settled in properly, and dare he admit it even if only to himself, to be near Sophia? Whatever her secret might be. While he was in residence at the house, nothing would harm either of them. He could say that for certain.

Chapter 14

After the Duchess had shown Sophia her upstairs sitting room and bedchamber, she asked Florence to take her to the room further along the corridor which had been set aside for her. It wasn't the one Ruth had slept in, but another which had recently been decorated so was fresh and new. It also had a much better view of the gardens which she thought Sophia would appreciate following their conversation during the journey from London. Cynthia said then that she would like to rest before dinner, and was happy for Sophia to spend the time acclimatising herself with the ways of the house.

Sophia followed Florence eagerly into the room which the Duchess had decided she should have, and was stunned by how lovely it was. Her first thought was that it was far too grand for her, but Florence seemed at ease so she assumed that she would get used to its opulence in time. She hurried across the carpet to the window, and was delighted to discover that it overlooked the rear gardens which were even more beautiful than those at the front of the house. She could also see part of the farmland belonging to the Carlfield estate, and the tenants' cottages some distance away.

All of which was explained to her in great detail by Florence, much to Sophia's pleasure. Having only lived all of her life in London, with its grime and fog coming in from the river along with the crowds, street sellers, and vagrants this was a very different world to the one she had left behind. Florence told her that the majority of the servants who worked at the house, also had families who were the Duke's tenants. Except for Mrs Pender, the housekeeper, but she had been with the family for many years. Her father had farmed for the Duke's father in his day, and when her husband had died she had been taken on as the housekeeper. Florence smiled then, and said her own parents and siblings also lived on the Carlfield estate. Sophia shouldn't worry about anything, as his Lordship and Lady Cynthia were both very kind, and charitable people. Treating their servants exceptionally well, unlike some others she had heard about.

All of it was like a dream come true for Sophia. Not only had she escaped from Lucas, and an unhappy marriage to Lord Dilley, but had found the most wonderful place to live which she hadn't even realised existed. She could even hear the birds singing when she threw open the window, which she did as soon as Florence had gone to arrange for her bags to be brought upstairs.

Sophia was equally delighted with her lace bedspread, the soft mattress and the fact that she had more than one pillow which she had at home in London. However an unexpected lump came to her throat when she recalled her old room, which she probably would never see again. But she was soon distracted by the looking glass, a highly polished wardrobe, and bookshelves which she immediately in her excitement hoped she might fill with books from the library downstairs. The Duchess had assured her earlier that it was well stocked with old, and new ones which she could read whenever she wished to. Although Sophia's heart naturally began to ache again for Owen and Hannah, she knew just how fortunate she truly was. There was even a delicately painted watercolour of the loveliest vase of spring flowers hanging above her bed.

She pulled off her shawl which the Duchess had given to her in the carriage and she had forgotten was still around her shoulders, followed by her shoes, and threw herself backwards onto the bed in the most unladylike manner. Making her giggle, as she was thrown upwards again once the mattress responded to her weight. Bouncing her up and down three or four times until she was satisfied, and had noticed the paper and pen left for her on top of a writing slope in the corner. She stood up quickly, and went to them. Remembering her solemn promise to Hannah that she would write to her, and that she would in turn tell Owen her news.

The problem was Sophia didn't really know where to begin. There was so much to tell them, but she did have some time to herself now to at least make a start on it. She wouldn't see Lady Cynthia again until just before dinner, after she had dressed, but which she assumed Florence would help her to do. So far as she was aware they didn't have guests this evening so it would be an informal affair, with only the Duchess and her dining together. Making it unnecessary for her to change into a formal gown.

She presumed too that she wouldn't see Edward again until after he had returned from France. Not knowing anything about the letter he had received, and sudden change of plan. Her heart sank when she thought of not seeing him for weeks, but there was little point in being upset about it. There was nothing she could do or say which would change anything. She needed to concentrate on making Lady Cynthia happy with what she did for her, and try to learn as quickly as possible how she liked things done.

In the end she decided to simply write a short note to Hannah telling her that she had arrived safely, every kindness was being shown to her, and that she hoped Owen and her were well. Adding that she would write again soon once she had settled in. She had just put the letter inside the envelope which had also been left next to the paper, carefully writing her best friend's name and address on it, when she heard a light tapping on the bedchamber door.

Much to her surprise after she called out to come in, a sixteen year old girl entered, and introduced herself as Effie. She said that she had previously been assigned to Ruth, and was learning from Florence how to be a ladies' maid. The Duchess had told the housekeeper that she was to look after Miss Barlow now if that was alright with her.

Effie was closely followed by one of the footmen who was carrying Sophia's bags, and grinned at them both before he put them down on the floor next to the bed. When he had gone Effie said, confidentially, "don't you mind any of the footmen or grooms, Miss. If you have any trouble with them you tell me, and I'll see that it's sorted out for you. That's what I'm here for, to make everything nice for you, so that all you have to think about is looking after her Ladyship. I'll fetch your tea in the morning, and make sure the housemaid brings you enough hot water to wash in, then takes the bowl away to empty it afterwards," she said, going on to recite as much as she could remember about her duties.

When Sophia asked, Effie said that she had been at Carlfield house for two years. Previously helping her mother with the younger children in their family. Her father was the Duke's tenant, and lived in one of the houses Miss Sophia would be able to see from her window. She admitted then to being very grateful to have been able to stay on the estate near them, since so many others weren't as fortunate. Also to have the opportunity to train, under Florence's guidance, as a ladies' maid. She said in earnest that she didn't want to make any mistakes, and risk losing such a good position. Her face had crumpled as if she was about to cry, and she asked Sophia if she had any complaints to tell her about them first. Giving her the chance to set things right before matters escalated to Mrs Pender's ears.

Sophia spoke kindly to her, and said that she most certainly didn't have any intention of complaining. She was delighted to have a ladies' maid, which she hadn't expected at all, and the pair of them would get on perfectly fine together.

After that Effie began to unpack Sophia's bags, and asked when the rest of her clothes would be arriving. Quickly changing the subject when Sophia told her that this was all she had. Effie continued silently putting away her shoes, evening bags, and the few hair ornaments she had along with her underwear. When she couldn't see anything else that needed to be done she stood waiting patiently next to the door. Until Sophia realised that she had to tell her that she would no longer be needed for anything else.

Sophia took the opportunity to ask her more about the arrangements for dinner, and Effie told her that she could always be guided by the clock outside on the landing. Since the house was run at regular times, when she heard the clock strike half past five, she would need to go to her Ladyship's sitting room. Effie would however come back before that, to help Sophia dress. Regarding the letter to Hannah she could either give it to her now, or leave it on the hall table where Jenkins would ask one of the footmen to put it with the other letters for the mail coach. Effie had hesitated at that point and told her that she hoped Miss Barlow didn't think she was being too bold but Jimmy, the footman who helped her down from his Lordship's carriage, had taken quite a shine to her. Making Sophia blush, and both of them laugh.

When Effie was downstairs again Florence asked her how she had coped with looking after Miss Barlow, and Effie whispered confidentially to her that she didn't have a lot to do. Since there hadn't been very many clothes to put away, and more weren't expected to be delivered. Florence was shocked by this, especially since she understood from her Ladyship that Miss Barlow had been a debutante and presented to the Queen of all things, so she thought at first that Effie was telling tales. Until the girl became quite upset about her accusations, and she believed her.

Florence knew she would have to warn the Duchess that her companion most likely didn't have enough day dresses and ball gowns for the number of social occasions she would be expected to attend in Yorkshire, which would be a disgrace in her opinion, and set the ladies of the ton talking about it.

Later that evening, after Sophia had changed into one of her less formal gowns and Effie styled her hair simply, she knocked politely on the door of the Duchess' bedchamber. So that she could accompany Cynthia downstairs to dinner. Sophia still had mixed feelings about the Duke's absence, and was beginning to realise how much she would miss him. Especially after them being in such close proximity inside the carriage for the last three days. She had become used to the thrill of being in his company. A part of her also objected strongly now to the fact that she had only just found a gentleman whom she liked a lot, and he had been taken from her almost immediately. Even though nothing could possibly have come of it!

Her thoughts were still in turmoil as she followed Lady Cynthia down the main staircase, and it came as quite a shock when she saw that Edward was waiting in the hall for them. Feeling her knees trembling under her gown Sophia curtseyed politely to him. While her cheeks were on fire from the blush which seeing him unexpectedly had caused.

The Duchess turned to her straight away, and said, "I have an apology to make, Sophia. Ned is going to dine with us. He won't be going away after all, and I foolishly forgot to mention it earlier."

Although Ned and Sophia both wondered why the Duchess was going to the trouble of apologising to a servant, neither of them saw the twinkle in her eye. After she noticed, with delight, the effect which seeing each other again had on both of them it was plain to see the pleasure on their faces. Making her hope that it wouldn't be long before they admitted their obvious attraction to each other.

Quite ignoring the fact that this still didn't mean Ned and Sophia would agree with her, the Duchess remained undeterred, firmly believing in love at first sight between whoever it might be, and that nature should be allowed to take its course. Moreover, what on earth was the point in Ned working so hard to become as rich as he was, unless he could have exactly what he wanted in life? She was also absolutely certain by now that this was a romance with Miss Sophia Barlow.

Cynthia Carlisle knew in truth how lonely her son was, because of all that business with Joey and Felicity, also that he could be quite stubborn. Consequently she hadn't been entirely convinced when he said that he would begin looking for a wife, that he was ready to do it. So it was her place as his mama to make him see sense, and this was what she fully intended to do. Sophia was beautiful, good natured, educated and well mannered without fault. The Duchess of Carlfield knew in her own heart that she had the makings of becoming the daughter-in-law she had always wanted. All she had to do now was get Ned to agree, and see what she was able to, that they were falling in love with each other.

Without knowing any of this was going through his mother's thoughts, the Duke took her arm to escort her into the supper room, and Sophia walked behind them. Taking a seat next to the Duchess she didn't fail to notice that Edward seemed to be a little upset, and her first thought was that Lucas had found her. Until she reminded herself that this was highly unlikely, at least not so soon after she had left London. Cynthia however asked Edward if he was alright, because he had that awful frown on his face. Unknown to her he was trying hard not to look at Sophia, or think again of how beautiful she looked tonight sitting next to his mother. He simply said that he was disappointed to have lost the opportunity of going into business with Lord Watson, and hoped that it was only a temporary setback. The Duchess responded by saying that only time would tell, so he might as well lighten his mood, and enjoy his favourite dinner which Cook had made especially for him.

Edward rolled his eyes at that point, and grinned at her as he used to when he was younger. Making her laugh. He was quite used to her treating him as if he was still a boy, but couldn't help wishing that she hadn't done it in front of Sophia. As it might well diminish his standing as a gentleman in her eyes.

Sophia couldn't believe how wonderful all of this was, in particular the way Edward and his mother behaved towards each other. It was exactly how she had imagined a family ought to be. Unlike her own where Lucas always told them what to do. While Owen and her were simply expected to comply with his every wish.

At that precise moment, Sophia dropped her soup spoon which fell onto the floor with a loud clatter. Her cheeks flushed immediately from embarrassment. While the servant waiting behind their chairs hurried across the room to replace it with a clean one, putting this on the table next to Sophia's bowl, before he picked up the offending spoon from the floor to remove it. Cynthia acted as if nothing had happened, since she didn't wish to embarrass Sophia any further, and continued her conversation with Edward.

However her clumsiness had made Sophia feel awkward, and overly anxious. Even more so because it was Jimmy who had picked up her spoon, and smiled cheekily at her when he replaced it. None of which escaped Edward's notice, or his wish to deal with the footman's impertinence which had now become a priority. So that both Sophia and he couldn't help feeling relieved when dinner eventually came to an end. Neither of them were capable by that time of dealing with how they felt.

When Cynthia told her that she wouldn't need her for the rest of the evening, as she would shortly be retiring to her bedchamber, Sophia politely said goodnight and went upstairs. Having also told Effie earlier that she wouldn't need her later, she undressed and picked up her journal intending to write a poem. She had drawn the curtains back, and was thrilled to see the new moon in the sky, surrounded by a myriad of twinkling stars. The perfect setting for a verse, and Sophia soon began compiling a new poem in the hope that it would take her mind off thinking about Ned.

Instead she wrote a poem about a handsome hero who came to the heroine's rescue on a moonlit night like this. Sophia didn't intend to show what she had written to anyone else but secretly admitting to herself that it was the Duke who had inspired her words. How she wished she could really call him Ned! She thought with a smile, as she blew out the candle and closed her eyes. Hoping that she would dream of him, again.

Chapter 15

The next morning Sophia opened her eyes thinking of Edward, and how he sometimes looked at her. Replaying every tiny detail of the time she had spent with him, so that she could relive it, and still excited by the thought that he wasn't going away. She hugged one of her pillows, daring to imagine what it might be like to be so close to him and even dance with his hand on her waist, before she told herself sternly not to be so ridiculous. She was no longer a debutante, but a ladies' companion, with a secret! Even if this had still been part of the London season, it would be very foolish to think that a gentleman like the Duke of Carlfield was going to show an interest in her. As a merchant's daughter, and now a servant. Trying to console herself she decided that she could at least think of him as Ned, since no one else but her would know this.

Sophia sighed sadly, as her thoughts returned to the reality of her situation. Wondering what Owen and Hannah were doing today, before she became stern again. She had to stay strong, carry on believing that all would be well, and try hard to help the Duchess as much as she could. She had so much to be thankful for. Everything could have been so much worse. She shuddered, imagining waking up next to the dreadful Lord Dilley, before quickly pushing the thought to the back of her mind.

Sophia got out of bed, and opened the curtains. It was too early for breakfast or for Effie to bring her tea, so she decided on the spur of the moment to go for a walk. It had rained during the night, making the garden look fresh and green in the early morning light, and she couldn't wait to explore. She would have plenty of time afterwards to wash, and style her hair, before she knocked on the Duchess' door. It wasn't as if she would be likely to meet anyone else out so early, so it didn't really matter if she wasn't looking her best.

She grabbed her journal, hoping that she would be able to find a quiet place where she could write in it. Hurrying downstairs Sophia was shocked by the sheer number of servants who were already going about their duties, as she made her way through the house, intending to leave by the backdoor in the kitchen. Despite doing her best to appear invisible, everyone she met seemed to know who she was, and greeted her by name. Even when she was outside there were others working in the garden, and tending the horses in the stables.

Realising her foolishness, and that she wouldn't be able to move about freely without being seen, she almost turned around to go back to her bedchamber. However the urge to explore her surroundings was too strong, so she carried on walking around the side of the house until she reached the front. Once again stunned by the landscaping, and vast lawns. From what she could tell, the last minute preparations were in progress for the Duchess' tea party later that day, which she hadn't been aware of until dinner last night. She assumed that Lady Cynthia would let her know things like this beforehand, once she had settled in.

After walking along the path at the side of the lawn, and taking another she noticed, she came to a walled garden and cautiously opened the old door set into it. Staring in wonder at what she discovered inside. The path had taken her into a very different world of vegetables growing in small plots of land, and huge glasshouses, which appeared to be filled with exotic fruits when she peeked inside.

It wasn't long however before she reached the rose garden, after she walked through another door on the other side of the wall. Sophia took a step back, unable to believe her eyes. She had never seen so many roses before, growing in one place. Their colours and perfume were enchanting. Feeling quite overwhelmed, she was relieved to notice a bench where she could rest for a moment. She made her way quickly to it, and sat down before taking her journal out of her bag. To begin writing a description of everything she had seen, with a note of her feelings about the garden and flowers which she truly loved, before everything in her imagination became lost. She was conscious too that time was passing, and she certainly didn't wish to be late for breakfast so needed to hurry.

Sophia had become so lost in her writing that she was startled when she heard the sound of footsteps nearby. She looked up quickly, and accidentally dropped the journal onto the ground. Her heart was thudding loudly inside her chest when her eyes met Ned's.

The Duke had just returned from riding his favourite horse around the estate. While he was taking him back to the stables, he recalled the bench amongst the roses which was the most beautiful place he could think of in the garden, and he decided to go there before he went back to the house. If he couldn't be with Sophia, his mind was craving solitude, and he had many fond memories of playing in that part of the garden as a child. He thought that being there again would soothe him, as it always used to.

The last thing he expected to find was Sophia, sitting on that very same bench. It upset him at first that he had frightened her by appearing unexpectedly. He could tell how afraid she was from the look on her face, until she realised that it was him. When he approached her she had dropped her journal and stared at him wide eyed, which only made him want to kiss her even more.

Nevertheless he was dismayed that he had intruded on her privacy. He stepped closer to her so that he could retrieve the book from the ground, and he brushed its cover with his hand to remove any imaginary dirt which might have been on it. He apologised profusely for having startled her, before he passed the journal back to her.

Edward felt a shiver run down the full length of his spine when Sophia's hand gently brushed against his, as she took the book from him. With the result that despite his earlier resolve not to do so, Edward found himself once again being captivated by the pools of light within her soft hazel eyes, when she looked up at him. A voice inside his thoughts told him that he should leave the rose garden immediately. He had placed both of them in a compromising situation, which could easily result in a scandal if they were discovered without a chaperone.

Edward cleared his throat quickly, and much to the disappointment of both of them he bid Sophia good day, before leaving the rose garden and her.

Chapter 16

Several hours later in the early afternoon, Sophia went back to the rose garden with Lady Cynthia. The guests for the tea party she had arranged were due to arrive within the hour, but she wanted to see the roses first. She said that the gardeners had planted several bushes in one of the borders last year. It was an old variety which the head gardener had told her was now in full bloom. Sophia had been surprised when her ladyship had taken her arm since she hadn't been in her employment for very long she didn't expect this familiarity quite so soon. Nevertheless she was surprised by how comfortable it felt, walking alongside the Duchess in the sunshine. Listening to her talking quietly about the guests she had invited, and at times confidentially, when she wished to mention something more discreet and would lower her voice.

She also occasionally asked Sophia for her opinion about this and that, which she only managed to answer vaguely despite trying her best to concentrate. The truth of the matter was she barely heard a word Cynthia had said once they reached the bench where she sat earlier, and Edward had spoken to her. Her thoughts were too full of him being convinced now that they both felt a connection between them.

Meanwhile the Duchess had realised that Sophia's thoughts were elsewhere when she spoke to her, and assumed incorrectly that her companion was worrying about the tea party, because she didn't have enough of the right clothes to wear. Although she obviously didn't know her background or anything about Lucas' frugality, as far as she was concerned this was a reasonable assumption to make about a young woman's concerns. "I hope that you are feeling more settled, my dear," she said, quietly. "You must treat this house and the gardens as if they are your home. Both Ned and I want you to be very happy here, with us," she said, pausing to use her hand to wave the objection away which Sophia was about to make, albeit very politely.

As a result Sophia was obliged to remain silent and not say what she had intended to. That she thought both the Duke and Lady Cynthia had already shown her every kindness, and there really wasn't any need for more. Nevertheless Cynthia was determined to finish what she had started. "There is however the small matter of your clothes, of which you will need a lot more than you probably have with you," she said, quickly putting her hand on Sophia's. While she insisted that she was not to object, since this was in actual fact a part of her salary. A small stretch of the truth which the Duchess felt was justified in the circumstances.

"We shall begin by getting Florence and Effie to alter some of the gowns which I no longer wear, and for the more difficult tasks which will be beyond them, seek help from my seamstress. Also get her to make you several of your own, so that you have some new ones. We are of a similar size so it shouldn't be difficult for the maids to do some simple alterations very quickly. As you know I already have a number of social events coming up, which I arranged before we left for London at the start of the season. You shall want for nothing, my dear, while you are under Ned's roof. He and I will make sure of that!"

She paused, to catch her breath before continuing. "I am sure that you will not wish to take this opportunity from Effie, to learn more of the skills she will need as a ladies' maid. Whilst she has Florence to help her.

Between you and I, Sophia, she was forever talking about the ladies' beautiful gowns whenever we had visitors. Until it was apparent that becoming a ladies' maid was clearly her vocation. I will also ask Florence to show her how to use some of the ornaments I can let you have for your hair," she said, firmly. Sophia appeared to be on the verge of tears. Not having experienced kindness like this in the past, and thought that a mother might well have done something similar for her. Quite forgetting that she had also been kind to Amy, when she had given a gown to her which she couldn't really spare from her meagre wardrobe.

Knowing that Lady Cynthia was right in her assumption that she didn't have enough different clothes to wear, Sophia said that she was very grateful, and would gladly accept her kindness.

93

Adding that she hadn't expected to have a ladies' maid of her own. So once again, she was very grateful for Effie whom she liked enormously. Not wishing Cynthia to think that she didn't know any better, she also made a passing comment then about her brother's frugality, and how she had struggled during the season to cope with the endless changing of dresses. When she didn't have the number of day dresses, gowns, or bonnets which had been recommended at her finishing school.

Fortunately she didn't get the opportunity to say any more on the subject, or be questioned by the Duchess about Lucas despite not mentioning him by name, since both of them had noticed Ned. He was walking along the path towards them, accompanied by a tall gentleman and two ladies wearing the finest of gowns, adorned with ribbons and intricate embroidery. One pink, and the other lilac so that they complemented each other beautifully. Even their tinkling laughter and the tone in their voices sounded the same, so that it was difficult to differentiate which one of them had spoken unless you were looking directly at her.

Cynthia smiled, turning her attention to them immediately. Welcoming them as her guests, and saying how delighted she was to see them again. She introduced Miss Sophia Barlow then to the Earl and Countess of Duxbury, with their daughter, Lady Lucy Exley.

Sophia dipped an elegant curtsy, and was immediately ignored by the two ladies. Whilst the Earl stared at her appraisingly for a moment too long before he looked away, but it was long enough to make her feel extremely uneasy. However she quickly reminded herself not to be too upset by this. Irrespective of how well the Duchess treated her, she was only a servant in the eyes of the ton. She also had to remember her lucky escape from Lord Dilley, the reason why she was there now, and that she no longer had the right to object to suffering such a small indignity.

Nevertheless Sophia couldn't help staring at Lady Lucy who had her arm linked through Edward's, as if this was the most natural thing in the world. It also clearly wasn't the first time that it had happened, if their easy companionship was the measure of it. Sophia could feel the rush of blood to her cheeks the longer she

94

watched them, and the sharp sting of jealousy erupting within her. Until Lucy caught her eye, and smiled knowingly at her making Sophia look away quickly.

Her heart sank. It was impossible to deny that Lady Lucy Exley was extremely beautiful, and clearly attracted to the Duke. Even if she had been of a similar social rank to her, which Sophia obviously wasn't, it would have been foolish to contemplate competing with someone like her for Ned's affections when she was obviously interested in him. Moreover he was by this time smiling politely at what she was saying, and didn't look in the least perturbed by her proximity. What Sophia didn't realise was that he was simply trying to fulfil his earlier promise to his mother, and make it appear as if he was searching for a wife. Even though his heart wasn't in it. Especially so far as Lady Lucy Exley was concerned.

After the guests had exchanged a few pleasantries with Lady Cynthia about a variety of inconsequential matters, all of them made their way back to the main lawn where a long table had been set up by the footmen, which they had carried outside from the conservatory. The maids had filled it with fine china and cutlery from the house, then added vases of flowers to make it even more inviting. Edward and Cynthia greeted the other guests who had arrived introducing Sophia so many times that she couldn't possibly remember all of their names. As if she realised how her companion was feeling, Lady Cynthia smiled at her and patted her hand, saying that she would soon learn who everyone was, so shouldn't worry about it for the time being.

Nevertheless a forlorn Sophia couldn't stop her eyes from following Ned at every opportunity, and her heart was filled with dismay when she saw Lady Lucy standing next to him, seemingly as often as she possibly could. Smiling, and gazing up into his eyes. As he looked down at her, and replied whenever she spoke to him but without Sophia knowing how he really felt in his heart.

Chapter 17

Meanwhile as Edward was receiving the guests he couldn't fail to see how uncomfortable Sophia looked, before she moved to stand behind his mother who had stayed beside him. Making him frown until he realised what he was doing, and tried to smile again. It was fine and admirable on the one hand for the Duchess to try to better her companion's standing in the eyes of the ton, but in his opinion an almost impossible if not exceedingly foolish task on the other, to attempt such a thing. The effects of which could easily hurt Sophia's feelings, and which already appeared to be the case. Without them even reaching the point of any malicious gossip and unpleasantness, which he knew took place in the conversation behind a number of the ladies' fans.

This really wouldn't do! However he wasn't sure Cynthia would listen on this occasion, or be able to see the sense in what he was saying. Once she had a fixed idea about how things ought to be it could be extremely difficult, if not impossible, to shift her from it. He also knew by now how much she cared about Sophia, so no doubt saw it as her place to champion her interests. Unable to accept that sometimes meddling really wasn't the best way to go about things, or that a situation couldn't be changed by her alone.

The Duke glanced behind him quickly to check that Sophia really was alright. His heart went out to her, as soon as he saw the look on her face. His personal view of the matter hadn't stopped him from appreciating that his mother was partially right. Miss Sophia Barlow was kind, and gentle. She didn't deserve being ignored or any other such vile treatment. Simply because she was a merchant's daughter, and not a titled lady. He didn't blame her in the least for feeling out of place. Maybe even hurt. He had seen several of the guests treating her as if she didn't exist when mama had decided to introduce her to them, and he assumed that she knew as well as he did that she could only expect more of the same.

Edward groaned inwardly. He would have to speak to the Duchess, and insist if need be that she stop what she was doing. He couldn't allow this to continue. If there was any chance whatsoever of Sophia being hurt even more, which there obviously was. If anything it was his place to deal with this. The niggling suspicion that his mother had also set her sights on Sophia becoming her daughter-in-law was also growing stronger by the day. He couldn't fail to notice how differently she was treated to Ruth in a lot of ways, especially in relation to the privileges his mother had extended to her.

The other way to put a stop to it, he supposed, would be to marry Lucy. The mere thought of which caused his heart to sink, and put the frown back on his face. He knew by now that it would never be a marriage for love, but simply one of convenience. Something which wouldn't make him happy. Although he would of course do his duty, and see to it that Lucy had everything in his power to give her, except of course love, which couldn't possibly be right. It was the most important element in a marriage, from what he had seen so far of others, and indeed in life generally. Edward Carlisle also knew that he was by now a little in love with Sophia, and again had a niggling suspicion that it was going to be her he wished to marry. Whilst the tragedy was he couldn't possibly do this.

All of this meant that the sooner he started a proper courtship with Lucy, followed by a betrothal, the better it would be for Sophia. If only to stop the Duchess from meddling, and divert attention from him having any interest whatsoever in his mother's companion. Even though he acknowledged that this was the last thing he really wanted to do, the situation was getting out of hand, and he couldn't contemplate seeing Sophia hurt any further. That equally wasn't right. However, getting his mother to see sense would still be difficult. He knew from past experience how awkward she could be when she had set her heart on something. She had already hinted quite openly that Lucy wouldn't make the best Duchess of Carlfield, and that she had concerns about who would be the most suitable to follow in her footsteps. Even telling Edward that she dreaded seeing all of the work his father and her had put in across the years come to nothing, because the young woman he married didn't have it in her. Or any desire to continue their charitable events, raising funds for the poor and needy.

The simple truth did of course remain that Lucy had a title, and Sophia didn't. It wouldn't be any good at all if he married his mother's companion for love, and they were then shunned by society. Admittedly he was a very rich man, but there were still those whom he knew would spurn her even as his wife, simply from sheer snobbery. No, Lucy was the woman he should marry! With her father's business connections allied to his own, he would forget all about love and put his full attention into making the Carlisle name even more reputable than it already was. However difficult his mother might find this to accept, and dare he even think of the arguments it would cause, she would learn in time to accept his decision. Getting along with not only Lucy, but also her mother, Amelia. Despite their different outlook on the world.

Despite trying to be firm in his resolve, Edward still couldn't help wishing that there was someone he could have turned to for advice: A father, uncle, brother or even someone at his club. The gentlemen he knew didn't seem to talk about their marriage prospects in this way or have a similar problem to this. At least not so far as he had heard. Making him realise how much he still missed Papa. Joey too. His old friend would have stood by him, come what may. Although the Duke wouldn't have been in this situation, if he had still been alive. Felicity would already have been his wife. Edward had to wonder then whether that would also have been the right decision. Especially when he was able to think of her loss now without pain, and imagine himself falling in love with Sophia.

Why on earth was all of this so complicated he was thinking when as often happened Cynthia's elbow nudged him sharply, and his thoughts returned to the present. He had become so accustomed to making perfunctory greetings on these occasions, that it allowed his mind to wander. Although it was again often the reason for the Duchess' complaints that he looked far too fierce, and brooding. She was asking him now for the second time if they ought to go to the tea table feeling highly frustrated by his earlier lack of response.

Edward apologised immediately, as he glanced quickly around the garden. The last of the guests seemed to have arrived, and were mingling now with the others. For a brief moment, he was very tempted to escort Sophia across the lawn to the tea table once his thoughts returned to her. Stopping himself just in time when he realised that this sort of thing was exactly what he had just been thinking about, and trying to avoid. Apart from the scandal it would cause if he was seen on the arm of his mother's companion, it might well raise Sophia's hopes that there could be something in the attraction between them when this would never be possible. She was also bound to overhear the shocked exclamations, and scathing looks sent her way. Not least from Lady Amelia, and Lucy! Although he wasn't certain how Howard would react to it, since the courtship of his daughter hadn't yet been discussed by them. The Duke took Cynthia's arm instead, and escorted her to the table. This seemed by far to be the better option. At least it also gave Sophia the opportunity to follow closely behind them, which was what she did.

Despite his earlier resolve, it was much to his dismay that he found himself seated next to Lucy. His mother also appeared to be disgruntled by this, if the whispering he heard her doing with Jenkins was anything to go by. There seemed to be some suggestion that the place cards with the guests names on them had been moved by an unknown third party. Edward also didn't miss his mother's accusing look at Lady Amelia, who was by this time seated on the other side of her daughter. Realising that he was going to have to proceed with his decision to appear that he was courting Lucy, Edward sighed and smiled at her as he began to make pleasantries. Asking after her health, and trying to look concerned when she told him she was looking forward to going into the house, since too much sunshine gave her a headache. Unless she wore a particular bonnet which was no longer fashionable, and so she disliked.

Edward looked at her face properly for the first time, and couldn't deny that she was very beautiful. Socially she probably would make a fine duchess, with such a haughty demeanour. However he did have the sneaking suspicion that his mother was

99

right about the possible fate of her charitable events, since Lucy's main concern always seemed to be herself and playing her part in the ton. He found himself once again unable to get a word in edgewise. While she engaged in the sort of mundane conversation which society expected from a young lady of her status, and to Edward seemed incredibly tedious.

Cynthia was directly opposite him, and she had arranged for her companion to be seated next to her. Ostensibly in case she should require her services during tea, but in reality not wishing Ned to lose sight of her. On one occasion when he had looked up, his eyes met hers. Sophia's cheeks had flushed deep crimson when, without thinking, he smiled at her and she quickly looked away from him. Not before he had seen the sadness in her eyes. In that same moment, Edward couldn't stop himself from imagining what it would be like to have her seated beside him, as his future duchess. He couldn't help feeling a sense of pride, and happiness, before the image was replaced with the stark reality of Lady Lucy's incessant chattering and presence.

He turned dutifully back to her then. She hadn't stopped speaking, or even appeared to notice him gazing longingly at Sophia, but Cynthia had. Giving her another indication that Cupid's arrows had hit their mark. Causing her to enjoy the tea and cake even more, as she took great pleasure in ignoring Lucy and her dreadful mother. And purposefully including Sophia in her conversation with the other guests, as often as possible. Until, with a glance at Ned who nodded, she had told Jenkins to announce that everyone would be very welcome to have more tea or take part in the activities which had been arranged for them. These included battledore and shuttlecock, and the tables were ready inside the house for card games, also charades if this preferred.

During the late afternoon Edward was alone with Lucy's father, Howard, due to some contrivance on the part of both of them as each had an agenda to pursue. They had been playing a card game for some time. It had suited Edward to be away from Lucy, and still be able to appease his guilty conscience that he was pursuing a courtship with her by conversing with her father. Also it had to be said that neither of the gentlemen wished to stop playing, without knowing the outcome of the game. Since Lady Amelia and Lucy wanted to return home to rest before dinner, Edward had offered the Earl the use of his carriage to take him back to his estate later, which Howard had readily accepted. The other guests had already gone, and the two gentlemen also believed that Cynthia and Sophia had retired to their rooms.

During the course of the conversation Howard mentioned how keen he was for Edward and himself to be in business together. While discussing the possibility of this and what it might entail, Edward was caught completely off guard when the Earl went on to hint at a potential match between Lady Lucy and himself, before saying quite plainly that if this had been going through the Duke of Carlfield's mind he would most certainly have his blessing to the marriage.

Edward wasn't sure how to respond initially, since he was still struggling with the necessity of abandoning his feelings for Sophia, until his manners reminded him to smile as if he was delighted by the offer. He thanked Howard for speaking to him plainly stating that it was preferable to the many subterfuges adopted by the ladies of the ton, to which the Earl had responded with a hearty laugh. Whilst the truth remained that the Duke still hadn't made a final decision on a wife. Since without revealing it, all he could see in his mind's eye was Miss Sophia Barlow, and her mesmerising eyes looking into his own.

Chapter 18

Meanwhile Sophia had joined Lady Carlfield in the drawing room. She was sitting on the settee, staring at the opposite wall at nothing in particular. A book was next to her, which she appeared to have been trying to read. Having insisted earlier that Sophia should go to her bedchamber to rest before dinner, once the guests had gone apart from the Earl who was with Ned, and that she wouldn't need her again until then. As a result Sophia was shocked now to find her ladyship in such a state. She had come downstairs again by chance to visit the library, where she hoped to find a book she could read to help pass the time, since sleep had eluded her. She still hadn't finished Northanger Abbey, and was hoping there would be a poetry volume instead which would interest her. Something calm and soothing after their hectic day, but as she was crossing the hall she thought she heard Cynthia calling her name.

She stepped across the drawing room quickly, to kneel down in front of her on the ornately patterned rug. Frightened because Lady Cynthia looked so much older, frail even, and she seemed to be exhausted after the day's activities but which probably wasn't surprising. Sophia knew that she had only sat down at the tea table, and been on her feet for the rest of the afternoon. Joining those playing battledore as soon as she left it. She had also walked around the garden on several occasions with different ladies, since Sophia had accompanied her throughout the afternoon. Walking behind of course, and not alongside as she did when they were on their own.

The Countess of Duxbury had at one point passed Lady Lucy's bag and her own to Sophia, so that she could carry them. Both of which were quite large, stuffed to the brim with what looked to be embroidery of some description, and were exceedingly awkward. The Duchess hadn't noticed this straightaway. Her back was turned after she had been drawn to a large purple flower in one of the vast beds. The name had escaped her, and she was trying her best to recall it. She was clearly annoyed by the Countess telling Sophia to carry their bags once she found this out, since it was for the maid to do and not her companion, which she was certain the Countess would know.

Without speaking her mind Lady Cynthia revealed her feelings in a frown which wasn't unlike the Duke of Carlfield's when he was displeased. She also made a point of ignoring Lady Amelia and her daughter for the remainder of the afternoon, so far as she could without it being a case of extremely bad manners. Giving Sophia instead her full attention, and concern. Hoping that she hadn't become overly tired by all the activity. Apparently also causing her not to hear the offer which was made by Amelia, for her to join them when they went into the house to play charades.

Not really knowing if she ought to call for assistance now, Sophia asked the Duchess if she would like to go upstairs to her bedchamber, and she could arrange for one of the maids to bring a dinner tray up to her. If she didn't feel like having a nap, Sophia said that she would be delighted to read to her instead. Secretly hoping that the Duchess would agree to this, so that she also wouldn't need to dine with Edward. Still feeling overwhelmed by the events of the day, and because some members of the ton had deliberately ignored her. Even gone so far as making it seem that she didn't exist during the tea party. It had been horrible at times, then having to carry the Countess and her daughter's bags. The last thing she needed now was to be pitied by the Duke!

At that precise moment Sophia wished Hannah and Owen were with her. She missed them both dearly, and had started to be afraid that she would never see them again. This train of thought was however interrupted by Lady Cynthia who appeared to have only just realised that she had been staring at the wall, and was asking Sophia if she would read to her. Sophia was relieved to see the colour returning to her ladyship's cheeks, so she suggested reading from the work of one of her favourite poets. Much to her surprise the Duchess declined, and said that she wished to hear something which Sophia had written. She would also prefer to remain where she was on the settee, at least for the time being. Leaving her companion with no choice other than to comply with her employer's request.

Somewhat reluctantly she picked up her journal, which was next to her on the floor where she was still kneeling, and stood up to take a seat in the chair opposite Lady Cynthia. Flicking anxiously through the pages, without seeing the individual poems she had written, she couldn't believe that any of them would be good enough to be heard by the Duchess. Until she eventually decided to read one of her nature poems, which Cynthia went on to compliment profusely.

However it wasn't what the Duchess had really wanted to hear. It was perfectly acceptable, and nice in its own way. With its talk of trees, the river, and clouds. Her aim in asking Sophia to read one of her own poems had actually been to get her to reveal her passion again, which she had seen sparked in the carriage when she had talked about her work. The words which came from her heart and soul, and she believed could also ignite the fire of love within Ned. She didn't want what had happened earlier to deter her in any way. As far as she was concerned she still wished for Sophia to become her daughter-in-law.

When the Duchess asked if she had another verse she could read which was about love, the romantic poem she had written in her bedchamber as the moonlight had been streaming through the window and she couldn't stop thinking of Ned, was on the next page of her journal. She did like it she supposed, and although she hadn't intended to share it with anyone else, it was only Lady Cynthia. She didn't need to know why she had written it, the words would never reach Ned's ears, and so she began to read:

> *"Capturing her heart in a swoon,*
> *While the stars twinkled high above*
> *The luminescence of the moon,*
> *A Lord and Lady fell in love.*
>
> *Unable to resist their hearts' desire*
> *On such a beautiful night,*
> *Or the light of the celestial fire,*
> *It was true love at first sight.*
>
> *Their kiss, warm and tender,*

104

Fate allowed them to see
What neither could fail to remember,
Or know without doubt, couldn't be."

Sophia's voice, which had been hesitant at first until she became engrossed in the words, tapered off quickly and regained its uncertainty. When she realised with a start that Ned had walked quietly into the room. Having been drawn to her by the softness in her voice.

Whilst all she could feel was embarrassment, and shame that she had been so brazen as to voice her thoughts in a poem she wasn't in the least surprised by the way he was staring at her, since she had bared her soul to him. Not understanding the impact of her words, or that they had touched the tenderest of places deep within him. Something which no other woman had done before, not even Felicity.

The Earl had finally left, and Edward had been making his way to his study when he heard Sophia's voice. He was captivated immediately, listening to her reading earnestly to his mother. Cynthia looked up at him, and smiled contentedly. Sophia had clearly written from the heart what she was now reading aloud. As she also wanted him to listen to it, she motioned for him to be quiet. He nodded, and sat down on the nearest chair. As soon as she had finished reading, Cynthia erupted into loud applause. Clapping her hands in delight, also because Ned couldn't have timed his entrance any better, and had heard all of Sophia's romantic verse which was wonderful.

When he also joined in the applause Sophia looked in his direction, and seemingly noticed his presence for the first time. Her cheeks flushed deep crimson. Whilst it was obvious from her face that she was in a state of embarrassment she muttered an apology then for not having a title to the poem.

Edward politely asked the name of the poet who had written such a delightful verse. It reminded him of Lord Byron's love poems. Making her blush even more that he should have placed it in such high regard. Even though he had guessed before he asked that it had been her, and when she was hesitant to reply, he knew that he had been right.

Before Sophia had time to say anything else, Lady Cynthia who seemed to have fully recovered her composure, interrupted and quite cheerfully told Ned that she had indeed written the poem. Quite overwhelmed by the sentiments Sophia had expressed in the verse and her talk of love, he couldn't help wishing with all of his heart that she had written it about him. It took every ounce of concentration he could muster to think quickly, and say something else that was complimentary. At the same time remaining distanced from his feelings, and what he wished had been a reference to them.

Leaving Cynthia delighted that everything was still going according to plan, and she hadn't had any reason to doubt it earlier when she was staring at the wall in frustration. Or to become despondent that the reaction Sophia had received today from the other ladies might well have deterred her from continuing to be very much herself. A truly delightful, and charming, young woman who was quite capable of capturing Ned's heart.

Acknowledging that if the way he was looking at her now was the measure of it, she had already done so.

Chapter 19

Sophia still couldn't believe it when Edward said that he had enjoyed her poem. It made her feel wonderful, as if she could achieve anything from now on. Although a part of her also remained doubtful that he had really enjoyed it. Surely it was more likely to be the case that he was simply being polite? Not wishing to hurt her feelings, by giving her the criticism the verse deserved. She also couldn't help hoping that he hadn't heard all of it, but as it was only short that was unlikely. If only she hadn't included the first couple of lines about her heart being captured by a lord, but other parts of it were just as bad! She wasn't a lady anyway, so maybe Ned wouldn't realise the verse was about them.

These thoughts continued to twist and turn through her mind. Until none of it made any sense to her. The only thing of which she was certain was that she had fallen in love with Edward Carlisle. There wasn't any doubt about that! Irrespective of his social status, wealth, and whether or not he told the truth about her poetry. Whatever else might be going on, he would always be Ned. Although never her Ned, she thought sadly. Finding comfort however in the thought that he couldn't possibly know she had written the poem for him.

Feeling the intensity of his gaze still on her face, she was by then almost speechless. Until she managed somehow to compose herself, and politely thanked him, albeit with a small stutter in her voice. Showing the correct level of modesty, she remained adamant that he was being too kind. All the while wishing that she hadn't chosen that particular poem, because of how romantic it was thus quite unsuitable for his, or any other gentleman's ears. But then how was she to know that he would suddenly appear? Sophia groaned inwardly. Why couldn't she ever seem to do anything right? Especially when it concerned someone she thought the world of, and the importance of both Lady Cynthia and the Duke liking her. If she left Carlfield house now she didn't have anywhere else to go. Only to possibly throw herself on Lucas' mercy, and hope that she could still marry Lord Dilley, a suitor who was nearly twice her age and completely vile. How could she possibly do that when neither of them loved each other, and she had given her heart to Ned?

Maybe if Lady Cynthia or the Duke changed the topic of conversation she would begin to feel better, she thought in desperation, and it wasn't long before providence came to her assistance. It was a huge relief when the Duchess mentioned the charity dinner she would shortly be hosting at Carlfield house. It had become an annual event, along with the impromptu talent show which took place afterwards, and she assured Sophia was great fun. However she wished to do something different this year, she said then, with a twinkle in her eye and a huge smile. It was going to be a literary evening instead. She might have mentioned it during their carriage ride from London. She couldn't recall, as they had talked about such a lot. Lady Cynthia asked Sophia then if she would be so kind as to read her romance poem to the audience after dinner. Her words were truly wonderful, and meant to be shared.

Sophia thought at first that she must have misheard. When her employer continued to stare expectantly at her waiting for a reply, she felt dizzy and the room began to spin. The reality of standing at the front of a large room, filled with the ladies of the ton and their gentlemen, had caused her to panic. To make matters worse Ned was by now telling his mother that he thought it was a lovely idea. Quite forgetting his earlier reservations about exposing Sophia to something like this. When the ladies of the ton might not be impressed by someone whom they regarded as a servant, being given the privilege of entertaining them, and react badly to it. Even though the standard of Sophia's verse, along with what ought to have been an element of kindness on their part, more than justified her taking part in the readings.

Sophia glanced at Edward who was still smiling warmly at her, and realised that whatever her feelings on the matter might be she couldn't refuse. As a result Cynthia was delighted when Sophia said that she would be honoured to do a short reading.

Shortly afterwards Jenkins announced that dinner was being served. The Duke took his mother's arm, as she chattered excitedly about the charity event. Sophia resumed her usual place, and followed them into the dining room feeling relieved when it was eventually time for her to retire to her bedchamber. However after accompanying Lady Cynthia to hers, and saying goodnight, she met the Duke unexpectedly in the hall outside. Making her apologies for almost colliding with him as she left the Duchess' room, he smiled charmingly and asked her if he might have a quiet word with her before she retired. Completely ignoring the fact that they were alone in the hall.

Unable to refuse even if she had wished to, and with her heart beating loudly, Sophia waited for Edward to reveal his reason for wishing to speak to her. Anxious that it might not be good news. Surely Lucas hadn't discovered her whereabouts, or was the Duke possibly going to terminate her employment? Sophia's thoughts on what she might have done wrong were however soon interrupted by him.

"Please don't be alarmed. I wished to thank you, Sophia, for the care you have shown to my mother. I hope that you have settled in well at Carlfield. If you need anything, or I can help you in any way, please come to me. I know how much the Duchess values you being here," he said, hesitating. He wished very much to add that, despite his earlier reservations, he felt the same but thought this might be a step too far at this early stage in her employment.

"I regret that my mother sometimes talks endlessly on a single topic," he said, uncomfortably. When he recalled the family history Cynthia had spoken a length about in the carriage, and reminiscences of his childhood. "I have also noticed that age makes her forgetful at times, and it's a considerable reassurance to me that you are with her. Especially when you are walking in the grounds or have left the estate" He paused again, trying to find the most appropriate words. "I beg your pardon for my inelegance, but should you deem it necessary to inform me of any matter concerning her health, I would be most grateful if you would not hesitate to do so,because I shall be very grateful to hear it. I have seen your gentleness with her, which is something I am not able to show her in quite the same way." He finished the sentence in a rush. Noticing how uncomfortable Sophia looked, despite giving him her full attention.

"Thank you for your confidence in me, your Lordship. Although I am still learning my duties as a ladies' companion, I greatly value my position here, and being able to spend so much time with Lady Cynthia. I admire the Duchess enormously, and feel nothing but affection for her," she said, remembering at the last minute not to call him Ned. Even though she very much wished to. Adding that although Lady Cynthia usually appeared to be in good health, she was concerned earlier by how exhausted she had been after today's tea party. Making it her turn to hesitate. As she wondered how much she ought to tell him, but actually finding it a relief to be able to share her fears about Cynthia staring at the wall earlier, which had seemed most odd to her.

Edward immediately looked concerned, and told her that this was what he had been worried about. It had been a huge shock for his mother when Ruth left suddenly, followed by the journey back to Yorkshire which wasn't very comfortable despite them being in his carriage, and a social event immediately after they arrived at the house. With more to follow. "Thank you for telling me. I will speak to her, without repeating what you have said," he hastened to add.

"I had noticed that she was becoming a little confused at times, and I wished to keep an eye on the situation. Although I equally didn't want to alarm you," he said, unable to stop himself from gazing into her eyes. On this occasion he was referring to his belief that Cynthia confused Sophia from time to time with the daughter she never had. Alternatively the other possibility was that she had of course been doing her best to matchmake. Both of which would have been improper, so not for him to reveal.

"I want you to be very happy here," Edward said, earnestly. Since he couldn't bear the thought now of Sophia leaving Carlfield house. ...Or him!

Chapter 20

Sophia tossed and turned throughout the night unable to sleep, and possibly not surprisingly, awoke the following morning still thinking about Edward. How he had looked into her eyes as he expressed his gratitude, and ardent admiration, for the way she cared about Lady Cynthia. However Sophia's confusion about the romance poem also remained until she told herself quite sternly that she must put all thoughts about it, and especially Ned, out of her mind. It was only making her feel more confused than she already was, and didn't solve anything. Nothing had changed. Apart from the Duke showing concern for his mother who was growing older, and appreciation that she was trying her best to be a good companion. As for the romance poem, there was nothing she could do about it now, and today was a new day, a fresh start.

Sophia looked around her bedchamber, with her head still on the pillows, trying to wake up completely. It was after dawn. She could see the sunlight coming through the gap on the edge of the curtains, and she settled comfortably again into the soft bed, sighing contentedly. She would have time to go to the garden before breakfast. This was the beginning of her new life. Admittedly she still had a lot to learn, but she was realising how much she loved being here. It was so different to what she had been used to.

Carlfield house was a joy to explore. She had found something new to wonder about whenever it was raining, and couldn't go outside in her free time, of which she seemed to have quite a lot. Especially when Lady Cynthia wished to be on her own, or was otherwise occupied giving Sophia what she had wished for. Plenty of time to concentrate on her own reading, and writing, which she still sometimes couldn't believe was happening. Even exploring the house, and how she now felt, had given her more to write about. So much so that her journal was almost full, and she would have to ask Effie how to go about getting a new one.

She also now enjoyed helping the Duchess reply to the considerable amount of correspondence she received, since she said that her eyesight was no longer as it had been when she was younger. Sophia was fascinated by the sheer number of people Lady Cynthia knew, from all walks of life. Making this task far from laborious, but very interesting.

She had been unable to decide what she liked best about the house. There were too many beautiful things to choose from although she had spent quite a long time staring at the Elizabethan four poster bed. Adorned with red silk from the Orient it looked magnificent, and fit for a Queen. Sophia intended to ask the Duchess, when the right moment presented itself, if Queen Elizabeth 1st had really slept in it, as one of the servants had told her. Portraits of Edward's ancestors hung on either side of the grand staircase in the hall, and throughout the house. These were magnificent too. The Duchess had also said that the marble used on some of the fireplaces had come from Italy on a ship and Sophia adored the glass chandeliers. The way the candle light sparkled when its reflection caught in the glass looked stunning. Carlfield was by far the most beautiful house she had seen, or visited as a debutante. Without wishing to be disloyal to her best friend or her parents, even Hannah's stately home.

The Carlisle family had lived here for generations. Edward's coat of arms was hanging above the front door of the house. They were old too, made of oak and very heavy and she had marvelled at Jenkins' strength and ability to open and close them. Similarly the footmen although she made sure not to stop, and stare at any of them. Most of all Jimmy, who still smiled and winked at her whenever he thought no one else was looking. She didn't like to use the front door unless Lady Cynthia was with her, and had become used to leaving the house at the back. It didn't feel quite as intimidating now that she had learned some of the servants' names, with Effie's help, and they greeted her kindly. Although unknown to Sophia there had also been some discreet whispering below stairs about the Duke's obvious attraction to Lady Cynthia's new companion, but none of it was maliciously done. The Duke and his mother were held in high regard by everyone at the house, and on the estate.

Nevertheless Sophia appreciated that being able to walk through those beautiful doors into such a grand house was a privilege, and one which made her feel like a lady. Instead of the servant she had become. She had been thinking about this a lot. It seemed as if her position in society was actually somewhere in between. As a ladies' companion her status seemed to be mostly parallel with Jenkins and Mrs Pender, the housekeeper, who treated her with the utmost respect. Yet she felt at times like one of Edward and Lady Cynthia's family members, or possibly an esteemed visitor, because of the kindness and consideration they showed her. Although this might be alarming on occasions, it was incredibly wonderful, she thought. Hugging her pillow once again.

What a change from how Lucas had expected Owen and her to live. Having a house like this to compare it to, along with how she spent her days now, she could see how mean and miserable he had been in his treatment of them. She appreciated that he certainly wasn't as rich as the Duke of Carlfield, but according to Owen whom she trusted implicitly, Papa had left them well provided for. She certainly didn't doubt that! Sophia shivered, remembering how cold she had sometimes been without the benefit of a fire, and how often she fetched her own tea and hot water from the kitchen and scullery. She frowned. How could she have called herself a debutante when that was the case? Whilst not having the gowns and accessories she needed to dress properly made all of it a sham. Even a disgrace, especially after being presented to Queen Charlotte. All because Lucas either wanted to save money, or make a lot more! The greater tragedy was that she had gone along with it. Not knowing any better and imagining it to be some sort of game, or one of the adventures she had read about.

Exploring Carlfield house had been a true adventure. She had so much now to tell Hannah. She was starting to worry about not hearing from her. Unsure what Lucas might have done to prevent her from writing, but that had to be absolute foolishness! What could he have done? Her more immediate concern should be Owen, and to a lesser extent, Amy. Both of whom were still subject to her elder brother's control. Sophia sighed. She was very fortunate now, to be safe under the Duke's protection at Carlfield.

Life had become a lot more exciting too, it had to be said, being often in Ned's company. Although he was preoccupied with running the estate, she often saw him in the distance with Tindle, his land agent. He also didn't neglect Lady Cynthia so was usually present to dine with her at least once a day, when Sophia would usually be there. Their eyes had grown accustomed to meeting. Even though neither of them was in a position to express his or her true feelings, it was still wonderful and telling herself to stop thinking about him was proving to be impossible.

Sophia looked around her bedchamber again, realising with a start that she thought of it now as her own, and Carlfield house as home. It was so light, and airy in the bedchamber, and full of flowers which she guessed Jimmy had something to do with. Making her blush at the mere thought of it, but her assumption was correct. He always picked the best blooms for her when the head gardener's back was turned, and he got the opportunity after he had overheard her telling Effie one day how much she loved flowers. However what Sophia also didn't know was that it was Cynthia who was at the heart of it all. Asking the head gardener to include her bedchamber on the list of rooms which would require flowers to be sent up to them. Once she had seen Sophia's pleasure at being outside in the rose garden.

Unable to settle her emotions and anticipation for the day ahead, Sophia decided to get up and go for a walk. Feeling that the fresh air might give her a better perspective on her conversation with Ned last night. It was a beautiful morning, the birds were singing, and she was looking forward to seeing the roses again. Effie was by now used to knocking on her door, only to find her gone, then returning later to remove the cup of tea which hadn't been drunk. As usual Sophia took her journal with her, and a short while later was seated on Edward's favourite bench in the rose garden, writing another poem.

On her way there she had tried her best to stop wishing Hannah was with her. She was desperate too for news of Owen, and Lucas. She couldn't write to her again until Hannah had replied to her first letter, and there was so much now that she wanted to say. Instead, she poured her emotions into her new poem, becoming so immersed in writing it that she was startled when she realised how long she had been sitting there. Gathering her belongings together as quickly as she could, and feeling quite flustered, she hurried back to the house.

Meanwhile Edward was making his way to the breakfast room, deep in thought about Lucy, and Howard's proposal that he should marry her. He was frowning to himself. Just as he turned the corner in the hall, someone unexpectedly collided with him. He automatically raised his hands and arms, which somehow found their way around Sophia, whose own hands had become pressed against his chest.

Both of them found the experience a pleasant one, once they knew who the other person was. So they were slow to remove their offending hands and arms, then step away from each other. Edward felt his heart miss a beat when he realised how right it had felt. Having Sophia so close to him. Whilst she blushed, and with a shy smile, apologised profusely for bumping into him unable to ignore the fact that she had been held by the man she loved.

In reality both of them would have been thrilled for this tender moment to have continued indefinitely, but propriety dictated that they move apart quickly once they were able to. Nevertheless they both stared at each other afterwards for a moment too long. Neither of them was able to believe what had happened, or how it had made them feel. Something which, had they not been completely alone, would have been deemed scandalous.

Sophia had never before been held by a man other than Owen. Only briefly then when she had been distressed by something or another, and he had been trying to comfort her. Before that Papa, when she had been a child, but it was different this time. She had felt a sense of dangerous anticipation being so close to Ned, and a thrill which she didn't understand or could explain. Although she knew with certainty that he would never hurt her. It was obvious that both of them felt the excitement and sensation of being very much alive in each others' arms not wishing for it to end.

However Edward also didn't fail to see the flicker of fear in her eyes. Reminding him of his concern that she hadn't revealed everything about herself at the interview, which he had recently overlooked because of her obvious good character and personality during the time he had known her. He immediately gave her a warm smile, to reassure her as he told her lightly that all was forgiven, and no harm had been done. He couldn't fail to see the look of relief on her face when he said this, which alarmed him again. As he knew for certain then that she was afraid of something, which shouldn't be the case when she was under his protection in his household. He wished he knew what was troubling her, and longed for the day that she would feel able to tell him. So he asked her if she was well. Before reminding her that if anything was worrying her he hoped she would come to him.

Before she had the opportunity to reply Cynthia appeared in the passageway, and said good morning to them both. Sophia apologised immediately for not going to her room, also not being as well turned out as she should be. She explained that she had been in the garden writing, so didn't realise the time until it was too late to go upstairs. Adding guiltily that this wasn't a good enough excuse.

Cynthia smiled at them both, ignoring Sophia's apology, and remarked on her perfect timing at meeting them both outside the breakfast room. They could now all go in together, she said brightly.

During breakfast, Edward couldn't help feeling distracted by Sophia, or stop glancing at her from time to time. Wondering why someone as beautiful as she was hadn't received a marriage proposal, especially since she had taken part in the season. In the meantime she was trying her best not to return his look, or remember what it had felt like being in his arms a few minutes ago.

When their eyes did eventually meet, their hearts melted in a passionate longing for each other.

Chapter 21

After breakfast Sophia joined the Duchess in the drawing room. Her mind was still spinning from her encounter with Edward earlier in the passageway, and their close proximity to each other. Blushing to even think of it again, that she had been in his arms! Something she didn't imagine would ever happen. However, she had to stop her imagination now from making much more out of the situation than there had been. She had accidentally bumped into him. That was all. Nothing else. No matter what her thoughts might now be trying to imply.

It was also becoming increasingly clear that she needed to be much more in control of her emotions, to make sure that her true situation wasn't revealed inadvertently by her in the heat of the moment. She was starting to be afraid that this could easily happen. She longed now to tell both Lady Cynthia and Ned everything. It wasn't her true nature to be deceitful, so she wasn't feeling in the least bit comfortable about it, especially when they were being so kind to her.

Even worse than that, the Duke would probably have refused to employ her in his immediate household had he known what she was doing. Whilst he now seemed to be entrusting her with his mother's health, and well-being, he surely wouldn't have done it, had he known her true circumstances. Sophia's guilt weighed heavily in her heart as she tried not to let her feelings show. She also knew by now how much Lady Cynthia wished to have a daughter-in-law, and here she was trying to prevent that! Tempting the Duke to look at her in the forlorn hope that something might come of it. Sophia's head began to ache. Unable to believe what she was doing, and what she had been thinking. She had no right whatsoever to have any feelings for the Duke of Carlfield. Her behaviour was disgraceful.

Lady Lucy Exley was obviously as interested in him as he was in her. A ladies' companion had absolutely no right to try to interfere in the progress of their romance, and it had to stop. Right now! Lady Cynthia would be mortified if she knew that her companion had left London to escape from an arranged marriage with Lord Neil Dilley, a peer of the realm. Sophia could well imagine the scandal all of this would cause, if the truth was revealed. Or even worse, if the scandal sheets became aware of it. None of them would be able to live it down. She was also starting to wish that she had never mentioned that she wrote poetry. The last thing she wanted was for someone to recognise her while she was doing a reading, which she supposed could easily happen. Yet how could she refuse, if her employer asked her to do it?

If only Hannah would write to her soon, she couldn't help thinking. At least she would be able to put her feelings on paper when she replied to her, and it would be as if she was speaking again to her best friend. Sophia had never felt so alone in all life. There was no one here in whom she could confide. A short-lived smile crossed her lips, but was gone in an instant. Ned had asked her to talk to him, but even he would be shocked if she now told him her secret. What was she to do?

"Is something troubling you, my dear?" Cynthia said, with concern, as she put a hand on Sophia's arm to attract her attention. Sophia had been staring up at the ceiling with flushed cheeks, which the Duchess thought seemed most odd and quite unlike her. After Sophia smiled weakly and apologised for daydreaming, Cynthia asked her if she would read another poem from her journal.

Although Sophia was reluctant to read any more of her work to the Duchess or anyone else, when her feelings remained out of control, she obligingly opened the journal to skim through the pages which were filled with writing. Until she found a few lines of verse she had written when she lived with Lucas and Owen. A deeply emotional poem about family and friendship, which touched on the loss of her mother. Although this was again a private matter she couldn't think of anything else which might be any better, and Lady Cynthia was waiting for her to begin.

The truth of the matter was that in addition to her present difficulties Sophia was also still grieving for the loss of her mother, despite her death having occurred more than a decade ago. As a result once she began reading her words aloud she felt overwhelmed, and tears began streaming down her face as she spoke:

> *"Nothing fills the gap she left behind*
> *In the yearnings of my mind,*
> *While I dream of the rose garden*
> *Where she now lives,*

In each comforting thought
And solace memory gives.
An Angel watches over her...

Causing Sophia to wish more than anything that she hadn't chosen these particular lines to share with the Duchess, but it was too late. Even to scold herself for her appalling behaviour. The poem wasn't even finished, nor the rhyming!

Meanwhile Cynthia, who was also by this time equally overcome with emotion, passed a handkerchief to her so that she could blow her nose and dry her eyes. Not saying anything at all while Sophia attended to this, and as she dabbed her eyes apologised. Saying that she didn't know what had got into her that morning.

"There is absolutely no need to apologise, my dear. I assume the poem was about your mother, and naturally her loss might still distress you," Cynthia said, pushing a stray strand of hair out of her companion's eyes. "Would you like to talk about what has upset you so much? I am not entirely blind to the fact that something has been worrying you."

Sophia could tell from the look in Cynthia's eyes that she was being sincere when she said this, and she wanted nothing more in the world at that point than to tell her everything, but which she couldn't possibly do. Consequently, after taking a deep breath and reassuring the Duchess that nothing was wrong, she began to talk about the few memories she had of her mother. Although she didn't have very many since she had only been eight years old when she died, and she had been shielded from it by her father. She said that she seemed now to only remember inconsequential things. Like them walking together in the garden, and Sophia seeing a frog for the first time. She had been fascinated, so reluctant to come away from it. Until mama had asked the gardener's boy to take it elsewhere. Not being quite so keen as her daughter on the creature.

Cynthia had smiled then, as she also had a dislike of frogs and told Sophia that she understood her mother's aversion to them. Sophia had hesitated then before quietly admitting that she felt her dear mama's presence, here at Carlfield, in particular in the rose garden. When she sat quietly with her poetry, and the flowers looked so beautiful. It was so unlike London, except for the parks which she couldn't visit every day. When she said that she hadn't been able to finish the poem, as she missed her mother too much, she burst into tears and Lady Cynthia Carlisle held her gently until she stopped crying.

Feeling equally overcome by Sophia's distress, the Duchess knew then that she had done the right thing in drawing her into their family. Edward and Sophia appeared to be as lonely as each other, and irrespective of whatever else might have befallen her, Cynthia was certain that Sophia had a kind and beautiful heart. Also that she wouldn't harm anyone from choice. She was too loving to do that. All of which shone through her words, and demeanour.

Cynthia was tempted to ask her a few questions about the rest of her family, and what had happened to them, but decided the time wasn't right. She had no wish to upset her even further. Moreover Sophia would have told her if she had wished to, and she felt sure that she would in her own time. So she decided instead to open her own heart to the young woman sitting next to her on the settee, and treat her as the daughter-in-law she very much hoped that she could one day become.

"I completely understand, my dear. Feelings like that don't just disappear with the passage of time. Your own mama would have been very proud of you, and your beautiful poetry," she said, sympathetically. "I also lost someone very dear to me, my beloved husband. It happened almost ten years ago, but I still think of him every day and wish that I could turn back the clock. It's still difficult at times to make sense of the loss. Why he was taken, when he was. We were so blissfully happy with each other, but then I suppose it isn't for us to reason why," she said, squeezing Sophia's hand, as she smiled at her. Wishing she could also tell her about the daughter she had miscarried, two years before Ned was born.

Although she believed that she could trust Sophia implicitly Ned wasn't aware that he ought to have had a sister. This was the other reason that she secretly longed to have a daughter-in-law and grandchildren. Wishing to fill the gap she had in her heart which the loss of her child had left behind, and unknown to her, Sophia had already started to do. Nevertheless, now wasn't the right time for revealing her own troubles, or fears about Ned whom she hoped would see sense. Not become distracted by Lucy Exley who, in her estimation, was full of nonsense and quite dreadful. Everything the Duchess despised. She was certain that Lady Amelia and her would go out of their way to make life at Carlfield a misery, if Ned married her. Whereas Sophia was everything Edward and her needed. From what she had said, the Duchess was equally certain that Sophia would be happy here at Carlfield, irrespective of what her life had been like before she arrived.

The trouble was Ned and Miss Exley did seem to be taken with each other, which wouldn't do at all. Howard also seemed now to be taking an interest in the situation, which wasn't unexpected since he was her father. All Cynthia could do about that was hope he wasn't meddling, and Ned wouldn't be swayed by interference from an older gentleman. There was also still the very important matter of love. Edward's father had been the love of her life, and as far as she was concerned this was a vital factor in any marriage. However hard she tried, she had been unable to see Ned falling in love with that silly Miss Exley in the same way, but Sophia was an entirely different matter.

Sophia and the Duchess sat quietly together for several minutes longer, whilst their own concerns went through their thoughts. Until Cynthia asked her to ring the bell for tea to be brought to them, with some of Cook's excellent cherry cake. She had smiled then, and said she was certain that it would do both of them good to eat a small slice of it.

Chapter 22

Edward groaned. This situation really was impossible, he couldn't help thinking, as his valet helped him to dress for dinner. Sophia was always in his thoughts when he wasn't with her. No matter how hard he tried to stop seeing her face, and dare he say it, replace her image with Lucy. He just couldn't seem to do it, and seemed now to not even be trying to divert his attention elsewhere.

In his entire life he had never been attracted so much to a woman, as he was to Miss Sophia Barlow. However the Earl of Duxbury's intimation that he should marry Lucy, his daughter, still sat uncomfortably at the back of Edward's mind. If he couldn't marry Sophia, that didn't mean he had to make a proposal for Lucy's hand or did it? Mama would get the daughter-in-law she craved, and a business alliance with the Earl would most likely be beneficial. He would have to make a decision on whether to proceed with it very soon. Even Lucy and her mama were clearly expecting him to reveal his intentions. Nevertheless, irrespective of the offer of Lucy's hand in marriage made by her father and not of course losing sight of how beautiful she was which had confused him initially, Edward knew deep down that his heart was still set on Sophia. She was the one he wanted to spend the rest of his life with. No one else. That is if he had been able to choose her.

Whereas if he was to pursue a marriage to Lady Lucy Exley, any sort of relationship with Sophia would definitely be out of the question. So he would need to ask her to leave Carlfield. Something which he was finding increasingly difficult to accept, but there wasn't any alternative as far as he could see. Despite his mother's nonchalant attitude to a scandal, and whilst he may secretly agree with her and not be in the least concerned about himself, he could never subject Sophia to anything like that. It would be highly improper, and very wrong.

A little later with his grey silk cravat tied properly by the valet and wearing his favourite cologne which smelt predominantly of bergamot, musk, and cedar the Duke made his way downstairs to the drawing room. He was standing next to the window, aimlessly staring at the rain and wondering why life couldn't be more straightforward, when Sophia followed his mother into the room. It took Edward a moment or two to catch his breath. Completely overwhelmed by how stunning Sophia looked in what seemed to be a new gown.

It was exquisitely trimmed with the finest antique lace, dyed pale lemon, with a drawstring ribbon of a similar colour beneath the bodice to accentuate her willowy figure. The pearls she wore were equally stunning, and quite valuable, he thought. Making him wonder briefly who had given them to her. Surely not another gentleman! The thought brought the heat of jealousy once again to his cheeks. Feeling entirely consumed by her presence the Duke felt an urgent need to know everything about her, and frustration when he recalled once again that this simply wasn't possible. Or his place to do so, other than if it was something which affected her employment.

When Sophia curtsied to him in the most enchanting way he had ever seen, Cynthia was smiling broadly as she watched them both, with a sense of satisfaction and pride. Unable to contain her excitement any longer, she said, "Ned, doesn't Sophia look charming, and so beautiful this evening? Please tell her that she does. She is wearing one of the dresses I had in my younger days. Florence and Effie have worked wonders with it. Don't you agree?" Not waiting for him to reply, which he was exceedingly pleased about, she went on to say that Sophia would most definitely steal a few hearts when their guests arrived and she read her poem later. Making Sophia blush, and look down at the rug in embarrassment.

Not for the first time, the Duke wished that his mother could be a little more tactful. Her suggestion that Sophia would steal a few hearts tonight really was unacceptable. Especially if she received the reaction from some of the ladies of the ton he feared she might. Also looking as beautiful as she did in such an exquisite gown wouldn't help her case once jealousy reared its ugly head. Given how much the Duchess clearly liked her new companion, he sincerely hoped that it wouldn't distress Sophia so much that she decided to leave Carlfield house. Admitting guiltily then to himself that this would be for his own sake, as much as for his mother's.

Meanwhile, Sophia was also feeling guilty but about her deception. She realised how much Cynthia had become attached to her, in all of the kindnesses she had shown. Even appointing Effie as her maid, and now, filling the wardrobe in her bedchamber with new clothes which were truly beautiful. Far too good for a servant, and someone whom the Duchess barely knew. Cynthia had insisted earlier that she wear one of her gowns for the recital, which the two maids had sat far into the night altering for her. Sophia also felt more than a little confused by all of this attention. It was almost as if the Duchess considered she was more to her than just an employer. Sophia's heart missed a beat. It was as if she felt like a mother to her, but that surely couldn't be the case. Her heart began to ache then, simply thinking about it, and the loss of her own mama. Finding it so overwhelming that her hand grasped her mother's pearls, trying to seek comfort from them. At the same time being very grateful for Lady Cynthia's affection.

It wasn't long however before all of them were distracted by Jenkins' polite cough, which was a prelude to him announcing the arrival of the Earl and Countess of Duxbury, accompanied by Lady Lucy Exley. Sophia felt herself trying to shrink into her new gown, so that she didn't appear quite as conspicuous as she now felt, and did her best to blend into the background. Quite forgetting that this wouldn't be possible, since she was still standing between Lady Cynthia and Ned. Not apart from them. Also because she did look absolutely stunning in the Duchess' silk gown. The Earl looked at her on this occasion with raised eyebrows, causing her to wonder what was going through his mind. Not being aware of the proposal he had suggested Edward make for his daughter's hand in marriage, she assumed the worst, and that he had guessed her secret.

Sophia paled as she lowered her eyes, unable to meet his stare any longer. The best she could do to get through the evening, she told herself quite sternly, would be not to overthink any of it. Despite how alarmed she already felt. Even worse she had sensed the tension within Edward, before he stepped forward to greet their guests.

The Duke was also at a disadvantage, without him realising it, and because he was equally unaware of what was going through the Earl's thoughts. The truth of the matter was actually quite different. Howard Exley had a penchant for alcohol, and gambling which was out of control. With the result that although the matter still remained relatively unknown in the ton, he was actually on the verge of filing for bankruptcy. Recently deciding that the only way he could avoid the disgrace of being sent to a debtors' prison was if he could persuade the Duke of Carlfield, whom everyone knew was exceedingly rich, to merge their two families by marrying Lucy.

In a drunken stupor one evening it had even crossed his mind that he could wager her hand on a set of cards he felt certain would win him the game, and a considerable sum of money. Although Lord Neil Dilley had been very tempted by such an attractive offer, and enjoyed gambling as much as Howard did, he said that he must regretfully refuse to accept the wager on this occasion. He had recently become betrothed. As it had taken a long time for his proposal to be accepted and the marriage was now imminent, he didn't wish to upset the arrangement. The Earl had been grateful for this refusal afterwards, since he subsequently lost the game.

Whilst in his more sober moments he believed that Amelia, his wife, had been going about the situation in completely the wrong way. His daughter's beauty was undoubtedly a great asset, but for a man like Edward there would need to be something more. The Duke would be looking for an intelligent and sensible wife, with whom he could also have a conversation in the evenings and at breakfast, before he was about to begin his day. Helping to keep him on an even keel. Something which the Earl lacked in his own life, and bitterly regretted. Feeling that if Amelia had been a little different, he might not have succumbed to drinking quite so much alcohol at his club in the evenings. Wishing instead to be at home, more often.

Hence his reason for staring at Miss Sophia Barlow, and hoping that she might soon be gone from Edward's sight. The Duke was clearly interested in her, and she was a great beauty, he had to admit albeit reluctantly. Given that she was part of Edward's household they surely would meet often throughout the day, increasing their familiarity, even though she was only a servant. Moreover the Earl needed his daughter's marriage to go ahead speedily. Since one of his main creditors was about to call in the debt which he simply didn't have enough money to pay. Howard couldn't risk asking Edward for a loan at this crucial point in what he saw as their negotiations about Lucy's future. Possibly making the Duke suspicious of his motive in offering Lucy's hand to him, and receiving a refusal on both counts. While he still had the upper hand at the moment, when Edward didn't have any inkling of his financial difficulties. The Duke also surely wouldn't be so foolish as to risk a scandal by marrying a servant? The Earl had business dealings with his father a few years ago. He remembered his admiration of him at the time, and he equally had an enormous amount of respect for his son. Despite this current subterfuge which came from dire necessity. Especially in the way Edward had continued to build his father's business after his death.

The Earl scowled. The problem was his wife and daughter. They had held him back in life, and were doing it even now. Amelia was far too absorbed in herself to be of any help when he needed it the most. She wasn't even aware of their imminent destitution. Whereas Lucy was extremely spoiled, expecting to have her own way at all times, and thoroughly empty headed. Unable to converse on very little other than the gossip of the ton, the latest fashion in gowns and bonnets, and the look a gentleman had supposedly given a lady which must mean a proposal would be forthcoming shortly. Quite ridiculous!

Furthermore, if Howard was being completely honest with himself when he was sober, one of the things he regretted the most was trying to foist Lucy onto a gentleman like Edward whom he did genuinely like. He would have difficulty changing her, but would need to if he wished to have any peace at all in his home. Not something he envied him in the least. Whereas from what he had seen of Miss Barlow she was bright, intelligent, well read and even wrote her own poetry. He could see the attraction there for Edward. Obviously for her the Duke's wealth and status, but he was also well travelled and spoke eloquently of the places around the world he had visited, which she would no doubt have read about in her books. This was what happened when women were permitted to read, and although he wasn't entirely certain that he should think of it this way, he actually believed that all of those dreadful bluestockings could well be right in asserting their wish to read and write.

Although neither Amelia nor Lucy would of course have any of this. Believing that being able to sew a piece of embroidery was the best way to a man's heart. When to be able to converse with him was of course far preferable. On the other hand Edward would make a fine son-in-law, and at least they would be able to discuss matters at length, which Howard felt would improve his life at home enormously. The Earl grinned when he noticed Lady Cynthia talking to Amelia and Lucy. Wondering what effect she would have on them, as she clearly didn't tolerate any nonsense. Those dreadful ladies they currently consorted with had been too great an influence on them. It really did have to stop, and however this sorry state of affairs turned out, he had come to a decision after drinking a considerable amount of wine that both Amelia and Lucy had to start reading without any more excuses.

Howard glanced at Sophia again, standing demurely behind Lady Cynthia and Edward. The three of them even looked right together, he couldn't help thinking in frustration. Even as a ladies' companion, she had backbone. You could tell that from looking at her. Although he deeply regretted the observation, he could definitely see the attraction for a man like Edward. Had his own circumstances been very different he might well have been tempted himself. A woman like Miss Sophia Barlow presented much more of a challenge. Not only in him having the pleasure of instructing her on how to warm a gentleman's nights, but his conversation too! Whilst for the Duke there would of course be the satisfaction of having to find a solution to the additional dilemma of how to avoid a scandal, if he should marry her.

The Earl of Duxbury could well imagine that something like this would intrigue the Duke of Carlfield, but not if he had anything to do with it. Howard raised himself up to his full height. He realised now what he had to do. He would have to put a stop to this, and Miss Sophia Barlow's scheming, before it went any further!

Chapter 23

Edward was seated next to Lucy during dinner, and following her mama's instructions on how to regain the Duke's interest in her, she was trying to talk enthusiastically about the literary readings which Lady Cynthia would be hosting later that evening. However when Edward finally managed to get a word in edgewise, and asked her if she would be reading, she stared at him wide eyed as if he had gone completely insane. The Duke was of course well aware that it was frowned upon in certain quarters for ladies to have an interest in books, but he hadn't expected to receive such a vehement response from her. Especially when this didn't equate to her having an interest in the rest of the evening, as she had been initially trying to infer.

Lucy said then that she played the piano to a high standard, again according to Mama and the guests who had listened to her recitals at home after dinner. They had also found her embroidery outstanding. She did admit then confidentially to the Duke that she had been disappointed by the Duchess' decision to change the theme of the evening from talent to literary. Since this meant she couldn't take part in it. Nevertheless she would be very happy to sit quietly next to him and listen to the readings. Edward decided not to pursue the matter any further with her, since he was already thinking about Sophia's reading later that evening.

After dinner, the guests were invited by Jenkins to make their way to the drawing room where the entertainment was to take place. Once everyone was seated Cynthia announced that Miss Barlow would be gracing them with a poetry reading to open the event. She also revealed that she had already had the pleasure of a private reading of her companion's delightful verse, so knew that they wouldn't be disappointed. As she was taking her seat again at the front near the stage, she gave Sophia an encouraging look, but she unfortunately failed to see it as her head was bent low. Not quite finished however, Lady Cynthia graced the audience with a beaming smile as she turned to sit down. Congratulating herself then on giving Sophia as much support as she could and still firmly believing that inviting her companion to read her poem would be for the best. Glancing at Edward once she began, the Duchess was heartened even more by the look of admiration on her son's face.

Meanwhile Sophia felt extremely nervous throughout dinner, and as a result had barely eaten anything. Her legs were quivering when she finally stood up in front of the guests. Especially when she couldn't fail to see that some of them were frowning at her. Not amused that they were apparently about to listen to a servant entertain them, and had been expecting much better from the Duchess of Carlfield who seemed wholeheartedly to support such nonsense.

Sophia had added an extra verse to the romantic poem she read aloud to Lady Cynthia, a couple of days ago, and which no one else had heard. Wishing to do her best, she hadn't been satisfied that the original version was complete without it. Thankfully it was still a short poem, so it wouldn't take long to read. Although it would still seem like a lifetime to her, and there were a couple of places where she knew she might falter. She had learned the words by heart, so that she wouldn't need to look down at her journal. Deciding that if she did encounter any bad feeling from the guests, which now seemed highly likely, the only way to get through the reading was to not take any notice of them.

Lady Cynthia had her best interests at heart in asking her to read, and it was an honour to be on the stage at Carlfield in front of her guests. If the Duchess had confidence in her abilities as a poet, which she clearly now did, it was up to Sophia to do the best that she could. Also reminding herself of how she had often regarded herself in the past as a bluestocking, and this was proof of it. Feeling very self-conscious she cleared her throat and began to read her romance poem:

> "Capturing her heart in a swoon,
> While the stars twinkled high above
> The luminescence of the moon,
> A Lord and Lady fell in love.
>
> Unable to resist their hearts' desire

130

On such a beautiful night,
Or the light of the celestial fire,
It was true love at first sight.

Their kiss, warm and tender,
Fate had allowed them to see
What neither could fail to remember,
Or know without doubt, couldn't be.

Yet when Cupid's arrows are shot
The wheel of fate begins to turn,
Who can then resist such a tender plot,
Or true love, dare to spurn?"

Unfortunately halfway through the last verse, she made the mistake of looking at the audience, and quickly discovered Edward staring directly at her. Sophia felt the heat rising in her face from the intensity of his gaze, and wished for the umpteenth time that she wasn't quite so prone to blushing. As a result she stumbled over the last lines of the poem, and was highly relieved when she had finished reading it. However, she had mostly managed to do what she thought would be best, and not look at the audience as she read. Instead keeping her eyes fixed on the portrait of Ned's grandma at the back of the room, Lady Emma Carlisle.

But it was as she had feared. As soon as she had finished there was a collective intake of breath from some of the older ladies in the audience. Exacerbated by what appeared to be a synchronised clicking of fans, denoting their obvious disapproval of her words. Hearing one of them whisper far too loudly that she supposed it could only be expected from a servant, to which the lady seated next to her agreed and flapped her fan even quicker. Whilst the two youngest ladies dared to titter, before they were firmly reprimanded by their mamas.

Leaving Sophia feeling as if she had bared her heart and soul to them, only to have it torn to shreds, and she was about to run from the room when Edward stood up. Clapping his hands in

131

obvious enjoyment of the reading and her skill as a poet. Calling out to the audience, and her, "bravo, Miss Barlow! Bravo!"

He was closely followed by the Duchess whose dulcet tone of voice called on the audience to congratulate her on having found such an accomplished poet, and charming companion. The steely gaze in her eyes dared anyone present to disagree with her. Being quickly pushed into it by Amelia, Lucy was by this time also on her feet. Clapping heartily, but all the while glaring at Sophia.

When the octogenarian Lady Markham began to speak again, to express her opinion that the reading had been quite simply unacceptable, Lady Cynthia interrupted her before she had time to continue. Sympathising with her that she must have been unable to hear the words of the poem very well. Much to the amusement of the other guests. Especially when Lady Markham asked the Duchess to repeat what she had said. Cynthia knew that she had again only taken issue with the poem because of Sophia's position, and not on its merits. She had heard a poem last year read by Lady Markham's granddaughter which had not been nearly as well written, yet still received a lot more applause.

Not to be outdone by the Duchess, the Duke of Carlfield had by this time walked up to the makeshift stage which had been erected for the evening by two of the footmen, and said in a voice which was loud enough for the entire audience to hear, "if I may have the honour, Miss Barlow." Then he held out his hand, with the intention of escorting her back to her seat next to Cynthia.

His smile, and the touch of his hand, were more than enough to overcome any doubts Sophia had about reading the poem. Also exactly what he didn't want to happen, she thought now that he did have an interest in her. When the Duke's sole intention had been to protect her from the unfortunate situation which his mother had put her in, and make sure she wasn't hurt by any of the mean spirited members of the ton. Although he wouldn't have been entirely honest with himself if he hadn't secretly admitted how right it felt, having her hand inside his own. Whilst once again neither of them wished to let go of the other.

Sophia hadn't of course been the only person to notice the Duke's interest in her. Lucy was by this time being consoled by her mother, and the pair were desperately plotting how to regain Edward's attention. The rest of the room was in quiet uproar, behind a mass of fans moving very quickly contrary to Cynthia who looked on in satisfaction, before she announced the others individually who were also reading in the first part of her literary evening. When they had finished she caught Jenkins' eye for him to let the guests know that refreshments were being served, if they would be so kind as to adjourn to the other room.

In the Duchess' less than humble opinion, there had been far too many older ladies in the audience who thought of themselves as much too old for love, and were undoubtedly jealous to hear it spoken of by an unmarried girl. When it really was the most natural thing in the world at any age, which Sophia had expressed in her timeless verse.

Apart from that, again in her opinion, everything was working out perfectly and as she had very much hoped it would. She was fully aware of her son's protective nature, that he was a gentleman in the true sense of the word, and had felt certain that he would behave in the way he did to look after a member of his household. Also, of course from loyalty to his mother. Listening to Sophia read her poem would also of course have been an excellent reminder of her intelligence, and that she most definitely had a mind of her own which she wasn't afraid to use. It was about time all of this bluestocking nonsense was put to rest! Why shouldn't young girls be as well read as their brothers or male cousins, and if she dared to even think this, write poetry too? She was extremely glad that Miss Jane Austin was now becoming more well read, Mary Shelley's Frankenstein had been published earlier this year, and there were others too.

For the next half an hour the guests mingled with each other, while they had their refreshments, and they could be heard discussing Sophia's poem. Also to a lesser extent the readings which came afterwards, and as none of these had been the work of a servant they were mostly better received. Sophia was relieved that no one paid her any further attention, as she resumed her usual place behind Lady Cynthia, and didn't utter another word unless she was drawn into conversation by her. However much to her dismay, Ned didn't leave Lady Lucy's side for the rest of the evening. Dutifully taking her arm from time to time, and bending his head to listen closely to what she was saying, as if he didn't wish to miss a word of it. Although she didn't dare say anything to him which was critical of Sophia's poem after seeing the stern look he gave other members of the audience who had done so.

Unaware of Ned's real reason for apparently resuming his interest in Lady Lucy, after a while all Sophia could do was stop herself from gathering the skirt of her gown in her hand, and rushing from the room in tears. Why did everything always have to be spoiled? Just when she felt close to him, and happy at Carlfield house. Whilst Ned wished with all of his heart that he could go to her, and leave the incredibly tedious Miss Exley to her own devices in which he had no interest whatsoever. Other than making it appear as if his heart lay with hers. So that there really was no reason for any gossip about a supposed interest in his mother's new companion, and the ladies of the ton would not attempt to tarnish either of their reputations. Believing that this was the most he could do, in the circumstances.

To make matters worse, in Sophia's opinion, he decided after the other readings had finished that he would read Lord Byron's poem, *She Walks In Beauty*. As a surprise at the end of the evening:

"*She walks in beauty, like the night*
Of cloudless climes and starry skies;
And all that's best of dark and bright
Meet in her aspect and her eyes..."

Deliberately looking at Lucy during the entire reading, much to Sophia and Cynthia's dismay, and without looking at Sophia as he left the stage. The Duke was fully aware that what he had just done may well be also deemed scandalous by those who were constantly looking for any topic of conversation which could be transformed into a perceived indiscretion. He hoped again that it would deflect some of the unwelcome attention from Sophia which was still apparent, despite the support she had received earlier from the Duchess and himself.

Unable to contain his feelings any longer, or stand aside and see the woman he loved hurt by others' opinion of her. He was however equally, and innocently it had to be said, blinded to the fact that Sophia might well be hurt even more by the withdrawal of his feelings towards her which she could easily have felt were increasing.

Although Lady Cynthia was alarmed at first by Ned's erratic behaviour, and that he seemed to have changed his mind again about Sophia, she decided not to be hasty and jump to conclusions. Not being able to pass comment on the morality of the situation, as this was far beyond her by this time, she did know her son exceedingly well. So wouldn't however be in the least surprised if this was a bold move on his part. Intended to cast the responsibility and blame on himself for any impropriety at the literary evening his mother had arranged. Apparently lending his authority, and support to it, in reading one of the notorious poems by Lord Byron, since this would be true to Ned's nature, and character.

In that particular moment, believing that she was right to assume this, Lady Cynthia felt extremely proud of her son and knew that his father would have been too. Edward Carlisle was in her eyes doing what he thought to be right, as a gentleman, protecting his family and the woman he really loved. However it might appear to others, he was a kind and considerate man in so far as social convention allowed him to be. Whilst Lucy and her mother, Amelia, were undoubtedly playing games with his affections. No doubt attracted by the vast Carlisle fortune. Lady Cynthia was also certain that Miss Exley would find another suitor before long. Someone who would be a much better match for her than Ned, who hadn't made a proposal of marriage to her. Nor did Cynthia Carlisle believe that he would.

She had to be right. It was love which mattered the most, and Cupid had fired his arrows. That was easy enough to see. Sophia and Ned were the perfect match. Although her heart went out to Sophia whom she thought must be dismayed by what was happening now. Wishing that she could tell her that this was still

135

far from over. ...Especially if Cynthia Carlisle had anything to do with it!

Chapter 24

The following morning Sophia reluctantly opened her eyes, as thoughts of the poetry recital came flooding back to her, and she turned over quickly trying to rid herself of them. Especially the worst parts of the evening when some of the ladies had obviously shunned her, but maybe they were right. She was a servant now. Nothing more. Irrespective of Lady Cynthia's kindness she had no right to tell them what a mere ladies' companion thought about love, and romance. It had to stop, she said to herself sternly, whilst she hid her face under the pillow in shame.

However it wasn't long before the touch of Ned's hand, and the way he had tried to save her from the vile comments and looks came back to her. Nevertheless it had been closely followed by his betrayal in what could only be deemed as a courtship of Lady Lucy. It was the final straw! Sophia felt exhausted, and utterly miserable. Also on the verge of a headache, after barely sleeping a wink again last night.

Until she realised, as she lay safely under the covers of her soft bed, that she had actually done something new which she never once thought she would. Reading her poetry aloud to an audience had been a different sort of adventure. Despite the poor response it had received from some quarters. Maybe she ought instead to think of her situation as an achievement. After all she did have a mind of her own, and it was hers to use whatever her current position in society. Although it seemed like a lifetime ago she had also once upon a time been a debutante, who was presented to Queen Charlotte.

From the little she knew about it, the other bluestockings were sometimes treated with disapproval, because of the belief that it wasn't ladylike behaviour to read and write books. A thought that made her feel a lot better. Except for Ned's behaviour things weren't actually as bad as she had thought, but her heart sank again when an image of his face close to Lady Lucy's came to mind. After what he had done, she wasn't sure if she could face him today or indeed wished to. He had betrayed, and hurt her feelings for him. It really was too much to bear.

However the longer she lay in bed Sophia eventually came to the conclusion that she didn't have any choice in the matter, but to carry on. She was at Carlfield under false pretences after fleeing London to avoid a loveless marriage which no one else here knew about. She had to remember that, and keep herself safe by not upsetting her employer. When Lady Cynthia was so keen that she should share her poetry with others, regardless of how standing up in front of an audience might make her feel. No! The only option she had was to do her best to appear as if none of this mattered to her. Ignoring her true feelings for Ned. Irrespective of how difficult it was going to be to keep them hidden, if she was obliged to look at him as a matter of courtesy.

Sophia threw back the covers, and got out of bed. Concentrating on getting dressed quickly she was soon downstairs in the hall, and on her way to the back of the house. Intending to go to the rose garden where she would at least feel closer to her own mama. When she heard one of the housemaids running after her, calling her name. Although it was unusual, Lady Cynthia had also awoken early. She was apparently in a state of excitement, according to the maid, and wished to speak to Sophia as soon as possible. By now the servants were well aware of her habit of walking in the garden before breakfast, and the maid was pleased to have caught her before she left the house. Being reluctant to walk any distance, since she had other duties to attend to.

Sophia made her way quickly to the drawing room where the Duchess had decided to have her morning tea. Enjoying the view from the window across the lawn, and down to the lake. Cynthia smiled at her, as soon as she walked through the door. "I can't get over my excitement at how wonderful your reading was last night," she said, flapping her hand at the teapot and an extra cup on the side table. Intending that Sophia should pour herself some tea, and sit with her.

"I have the most wonderful news for you!" She said, brightly. "One of my closest friends was also very impressed by your verse.

138

Despite its brevity, Lady Moreton was sufficiently intrigued by the words to want to hear more, and sent an urgent message to me this morning. Saying that she had written it as soon as she opened her eyes. Being in the same state of excitement as myself, she couldn't wait to tell me what she had decided must be done."

Lady Cynthia paused to catch her breath, before she announced that her dear friend wished to publish a small volume of Sophia's best work, which she would like sent to her without delay. Giving her the opportunity to decide which lines ought to be included, and of course, to check that they were of a comparable standard to the ones she had heard. Which naturally they would be the Duchess had enthused, clapping her hands in delight.

Sophia couldn't help staring at her with wide eyes. Unable to believe at first that she was the recipient of such good fortune. "Thank you from the bottom of my heart, Lady Cynthia. I never expected anything like this would happen. It's wonderful, but I am worried that my words won't be sufficiently well written for publication," she couldn't help adding, as she sat down with her tea. The Duchess ignored her concerns with a wave of her hand, and carried on sipping from her own cup.

"I never once imagined that my poems would be in a book, going to be read by other people," she said, shaking her head in amazement. Also that someone else whom she didn't know seemed to have faith in her abilities as a poet.

What she didn't realise was that the Duchess had actually spoken to Lady Moreton last night, when Sophia was otherwise engaged, and asked if she would be able to persuade her husband to help. Both of them being of the same mind that it was vital to manage the gentlemen in their lives whenever they needed to. Furthermore, the behaviour of some of the ladies of the ton was on occasions most unacceptable, if not appalling. As it had been at Cynthia's literary evening.

Lady Moreton was intrigued by her old friend's request, and readily agreed. She had genuinely enjoyed listening to Sophia's verse which she thought she had read admirably, and would have liked to hear more of it. The matter had been progressed by her during the carriage ride home with Lord Moreton, and later, when they retired to their bedchamber. Until Lady Moreton had secured a promise from him that he would indeed be prepared to make his printing press available for a small volume of work by Miss Sophia Barlow. Although he did have to add a caveat regarding the other poems submitted by her being of a similar quality and which, in his wife's words, would of course be the case.

"I understand completely that this is a lot for you to take in, Sophia, and you will of course have plenty of time to think about it," the Duchess said, putting her cup on the table and standing up. "We can talk more later, and if you have any ideas by then of the other poems you would like to include in your book. However I must leave you now, my dear, to enjoy your tea. I have a meeting with the housekeeper to discuss the final preparations for the soiree this evening."

Sophia thanked the Duchess again for her kindness. Deciding to drink the hot tea as quickly as she could, before making her way to the garden as she had originally intended. It would be possible for her to think about everything on the way there, and allow the shock of what had happened to settle. She was about to leave the room when Jenkins stepped inside, holding a highly polished silver tray. She couldn't help smiling when she saw the sealed letter on it which was addressed to her, and that it really was from Hannah as she hoped it might be. She recognised her handwriting immediately.

Despite a pressing need to learn what had been happening in London, Sophia decided to postpone the pleasure of reading it until she was seated comfortably on her favourite bench in the rose garden. Anxious too that if she remained in the drawing room Lady Cynthia, or even Ned, might disturb her. Either of them could easily ask about her correspondent, or for further details of Hannah 's background, which she had so far been able to avoid revealing. Nevertheless, Sophia was in for another surprise. The contents of the letter weren't as she had expected. She felt her stomach twisting into knots when she tore it open as soon as she had sat down on the bench, and began eagerly to read the few lines inside.

Hannah told her in the first line that Lucas was furious about her disappearance. Even worse than that, Owen had also said he intended to stop at nothing until he had tracked her down. Hannah was relieved, and delighted to learn from her letter that Sophia had arrived safely in Yorkshire and all was well. In the circumstances however Owen believed that the best and safest option would be for them not to correspond with each other, at least for the time being, and Hannah wished to abide by his opinion.

Sophia had to summon all of her willpower not to burst into tears when she had finished reading the letter for the second time. Making certain she hadn't missed anything important in her haste to read it immediately. She couldn't help feeling abandoned by her brother, and best friend. It took her a few minutes to appreciate that they had only said it wouldn't be advisable for them to write to each other, to keep her safe. It would be easy enough for someone like Lucas to intercept their letters, and discover her whereabouts from them.

The added realisation then, that everything she had grown to love in the last few weeks might soon be taken from her, was unbearable. Sophia truly believed in that particular moment that she might never see Ned again, or Lady Cynthia. After possibly being forcibly removed from Carlfield house by her older brother. Her whole world felt as if it was falling down around her.

Chapter 25

Meanwhile Edward and the Earl of Duxbury had gone horseback riding on the Carlfield estate. When they reached the river the Duke dismounted, and invited Howard to join him. So that the horses could rest for a few minutes, and they could take in the view. This was another of the Duke's favourite places on the estate. The countryside was lush and green, while the sound of the water travelling across the rocks felt soothing whenever he came here. His thoughts soon turned to Sophia. Unable to stop himself from wondering whether she had been here, before he realised that it would be too far for her to walk on her own. Wishing then that he could accompany her, but which would of course be impossible.

Nevertheless she would love everything about it, as he did. Then no doubt write a few lines of lovely verse in the journal she carried everywhere about nature this time, he thought sadly. Trying also to put the image out of his mind of her standing bravely in front of an audience at his mother's instigation, apparently not being afraid to read her words, and which had impressed him immensely. Increasing the stirring of love he already felt for her, he realised. As he turned back to Howard who was by this time staring uneasily at the ground, and not as Edward had imagined he would be, at the view.

It had been easy to guess the underlying reason for the Earl requesting that they should meet this morning. Edward had suggested Carlfield so that he could take his favourite horse out, but even though he had enjoyed the ride his heart sank, now that they were on their own. It might have made the conversation he was about to have with his companion a little easier, if they had been with other people. Maybe at one of their clubs, and Howard didn't waste any time. He asked Edward straight away if he had given any more thought to making a proposal for Lucy's hand in marriage.

Without knowing the real reason why the Earl was intent on a betrothal being made as soon as possible, Edward still thought that it would be foolish not to consider marrying his daughter. Primarily to please his mother, and strengthen his business connections. Just then however, a different image of Sophia came to mind which he found impossible to ignore. She was staring directly at him, and smiling sadly as she looked into his eyes. He somehow felt that she was reminding him strongly of his desire to marry for love, as his parents had done. So that the truth of the matter came rushing back to him. Irrespective of his beautiful surroundings, and belief that being married to Lady Lucy would be the most sensible option, the Duke simply couldn't deny his feelings for his mother's companion which went far beyond a simple attraction. Miss Sophia Barlow was the woman he wished to marry. Had he any choice in the matter.

Howard looked the Duke in the eye, and said that he had been intending to allow him to take as much time as he needed before reaching a decision. However, following the events at Lady Cynthia's literary evening along with the gossip he had been informed by his wife was continuing across the salons in the ton and elsewhere, the matter had clearly escalated. So that having the luxury of time was no longer possible. Even worse was the suggestion being made that a scandal had taken place at Lady Cynthia's soiree, which didn't only include the Duke and a possible liaison with his mother's companion, but also his own daughter. Lady Amelia had assured him that this was already being repeated, and considered, by the most reliable sources of gossip.

Furthermore, having been present on the evening concerned, the Earl could quite easily see how all this had come about. However he couldn't stand back now, and see both his own good name and his daughter's tarnished by the Duke's seemingly inappropriate behaviour. It was, to put it bluntly, totally inexcusable! Also a matter of some surprise, that a titled gentleman like himself should have clearly become smitten with a mere ladies' companion. Although he did of course understand how this had happened, given that Miss Barlow was a great beauty. He also appreciated Edward's attempts at rectifying his mistake after the reading. When he had returned to Lucy's side, and focused his entire attention on her which had been admirable. The Earl smiled lasciviously then, and tried to make light of the

143

seriousness of what had occurred. Repeating that between the two of them, he could certainly understand the attraction of a beautiful woman like Miss Barlow.

Whilst Howard's final comment had the opposite effect to the one desired by him, in that Edward soon felt the heat of jealousy coursing through him, which he tried his best to ignore. It wouldn't do any good to respond in the way he wished to. Namely, that it was highly improper for a married gentleman like the Earl of Duxbury to show such an interest in Miss Barlow. Had Edward been a violent man who believed that it would solve his current dilemma, his inclination might well have been to challenge the Earl to a duel. Although this was a matter of honour, he also wasn't entirely certain that he had any right to pursue it. Only from the point of view that his mother's companion was in his employment, so protection. He could however imagine the gossip about him defending a servant's virtue. Especially since fighting a duel involved a risk to life and limb, but he could tell from the look on Howard's face that he would have to do something. It wouldn't be possible to delay making a decision any longer, regarding whether or not he was prepared to marry Lucy.

In desperation and just to see an end to the matter, it did cross Edward's mind to make a proposal immediately, but his heart held him back. He simply couldn't do it. Marrying Lucy would be wrong when he was in love with Sophia. It was also unlikely that there would be a good enough reason to withdraw the proposal later, so he would be trapped. To do it then would cause more of a scandal and difficult situation than he was already in.

Moreover he also still wasn't entirely convinced that his mother would accept Lucy as her daughter-in-law, or the fact that she would be related by marriage to Lady Amelia, both of whom she clearly despised. Not only that, but he would be obliged to terminate Sophia's employment, since this would be expected probably also by Lucy. Whilst if he did make a proposal to Sophia, his earlier thoughts on the outcome of this remained the same. It would be done for love but, unlike the Duchess, he wasn't entirely convinced that he would be able to protect her from the unpleasantness of being shunned by some of the other ladies.

Including Lucy, and her mother, he anticipated. Nonetheless his heart reminded him again, that this was what he really wanted to do.

Apart from the birds singing and the sound of the river flowing across the rocks, neither the Earl nor the Duke had spoken again. Until Howard decided that he had to break the silence. Ultimately, he wasn't in any position to press Edward any further than he had done, and risk completely losing the marriage proposal. Seeing the indecision in his eyes, he reluctantly said that he would give Edward three more days. Although he didn't of course reveal it, this was the deadline he had to pay his creditor. Leaving him in the awkward position of having to ask his future son-in-law for a loan immediately after he had consented to his marriage to Lucy. Meanwhile, he would have to speak more sternly to his wife, impressing upon her the need to ensure that Lucy did everything in her power to capture the Duke's heart. Instructing her in the art of using as many of her womanly wiles as possible, to gain a proposal naturally from him. This would strengthen the bond between Edward and her, putting Miss Barlow well and truly out of the running. It would also encourage the likelihood of the Duke agreeing more easily to pay off her father's debts, and prevent another scandal occurring in which he had unwittingly become involved.

Having reached an agreement of sorts, the two gentlemen finished their ride and Edward returned to Carlfield house to spend the rest of the day in his study. Although it had to be said that he didn't get a lot of work done, since his thoughts remained focused on whom he should marry. After changing for dinner, he joined Lady Cynthia and Sophia in the ballroom that evening.

The Duke's heart immediately began to race when he saw Sophia, and their eyes met. She looked even more beautiful in the pure white gown she had worn to be presented to the Queen, which he hadn't seen before. He couldn't fail to notice that it had attracted a number of envious glances from the ladies, and looks of admiration from certain gentlemen. Candlelight twinkled in the large mirrors on the walls. Making the ballroom appear as if it was

145

inside a myriad of stars, as the dancers twirled across the centre of it.

However, much to his dismay, he also couldn't fail to notice the sadness in Sophia's smile. He wished that he could talk to her about what had been happening between them without it being spoken of, but he knew that he couldn't. Some topics of conversation really were forbidden. Even if this was because they were simply too difficult to be mentioned. Asking her what was wrong would be crossing that invisible line, and pointless, since he already knew. He could see the love which was also in her eyes.

Edward tore himself away from gazing at her when the Earl and Countess of Duxbury, accompanied by Lady Lucy, approached them. Causing Sophia to move and stand behind the Duchess, much to Lady Cynthia's and his annoyance. Whilst the Duke felt as if he was left without any choice, other than to politely request one of Lady Lucy's dance sets. Since this would be expected. He couldn't help but notice that she seemed to be more forthright than usual. Even though they had only been in each other's company for a couple of minutes she had already apologised for touching his hand accidentally. When Edward was certain that this had been contrived, especially when she did it a second time, and Lucy's fingers lingered on his hand. He tried not to recoil from her touch to offend her, but found it difficult not to. Especially when they were in such close proximity on the dance floor a short while later, twirling around the ballroom.

Edward caught a glimpse of sadness on Sophia's face. She was still standing discreetly behind his mother whilst the latter was engrossed in conversation with Lady Barton, another one of her friends. He couldn't bear it. Sophia was standing by herself, no doubt feeling hurt and very much alone. Looking back at Lucy, Edward realised that he would never be able to love her. His heart belonged to Sophia. ...It always would.

Chapter 26

Sophia was still thinking about the letter which she had received from Hannah, wondering if there was anything at all she could do about the situation, when she was approached by Edward. After he had finished dancing with Lucy, and returned her to her mother. Sophia's heart missed a beat under the intensity of his gaze. Making her feel as if she ought to run from him, but knowing equally that this was the very last thing she wanted to do. Nevertheless it still came as a complete surprise when he bowed, and asked if he might have the honour of sharing the next dance set with her.

Sophia took a deep breath, before she found the courage to tell him that in the circumstances she didn't think dancing together would be entirely appropriate.

Edward frowned. He was taken aback, not expecting her refusal. Although he was of course able to understand her reluctance on the one hand, he couldn't bear the thought of allowing her to seemingly end what had started between them. So he reminded her in as dignified a manner as he could, that the eyes of the majority of the guests would be on them. If he had to walk away because she had obviously refused his offer, it would be duly noted by those dreadful people whose way of life was to dwell on such things. Adding in frustration that it was generally considered to be the height of poor manners to decline the host's request. Surely her refusal would cause as much gossip, possibly even more, than if she simply took his hand now which he was still offering to her!

The Duke hesitated, before he smiled sadly at her. Unable to hide the truth of his own feelings, his eyes softened as he continued to gaze into hers which she didn't fail to see. Before he told her that he simply wished to dance with her, and couldn't see why it should be wrong. Although Sophia was left with no choice other than to apologise and graciously accept his hand by placing her own inside it, from the tender way she looked at him Ned knew that she wished to be in his arms again.

She totally ignored the looks of disdain cast in her direction which she already knew would be forthcoming, as Edward led her onto the dance floor. None of which stopped her from feeling a pleasurable sensation travel down the length of her spine when he put his hand on her lower back. It was gently done, but with a firmness that she believed indicated she would be safe from harm in his strong arms. As he twirled her expertly around the ballroom, never once missing a step or treading on her toes as some of the other gentlemen had done when she was a debutante. Sophia's thoughts were filled with how this would only add to the scandal which she believed had already begun. Based on Ned's and her impropriety at the poetry recital, and that neither of them seemed capable now of stopping it from happening. The attraction between them was too strong for that. She sighed inwardly. Trying to savour every precious moment of his proximity whilst her heart was screaming at her that she was a fool. This had to end. Now! Whether she wished it to or not. It was simply what happened in situations like Ned, and hers.

Sensing the tension within her as he held her, and anticipating that her feelings would more than likely mirror his own, Ned became determined to put her more at ease so he began to talk about books and literature. So far as their dance steps permitted it. Considering this to be a safe enough topic of conversation, and one which was dear to both their hearts. It also of course meant that he had to bend his head lower to her face, so that she could hear what he said. Creating an even greater closeness between them, and a more intimate image for those who were scrutinising every scandalous detail. Resulting in some very quick flapping of fans indeed.

Sophia soon learned that Edward also had a passion for reading, which came as a surprise since he hadn't mentioned it before and she couldn't recall seeing him with a book in his hand. It transpired that he really did enjoy poetry, and admitted that he liked to read before he fell asleep at night. Delighting Sophia that she was the recipient of such an intimate detail, and leaving him wondering as soon as he had said it if he should have gone so far as

148

to tell her this. Causing his grip on her hand to tighten a little, making the revelation even more exciting.

Furthermore not only did Ned have a library at his house in Yorkshire, but kept a smaller one at the townhouse in London. He was in the habit of visiting the booksellers there to buy the latest publications, which he would usually have sent on to Carlfield since this was where he spent the most time. He told Sophia then that this was a topic they must discuss more at length, and that he was looking forward to hearing what she liked to read. Knowing already from Lady Cynthia that Sophia had visited the circulating library in London whenever she could, to borrow books. Something which he hadn't so far had the time to do but finding it easier to visit the booksellers near his favourite club. Without telling Sophia, this had always been to his mother's regret. Feeling certain before he knew her companion, that there was every chance he would meet the right young lady for him among the bookshelves. Since the circulating library wasn't only a place to borrow books, but somewhere to be seen during the season, and meet the right people which she wasn't entirely certain Ned was aware of.

He also said with a twinkle in his eye that he was looking forward to hearing a lot more of Sophia's verse, and as he believed that works of art should be shared with others. Pleased to see the look of alarm which crossed her face initially change to relief, then delight. Remarking to himself that the adage was true: Our eyes really were the windows of the soul.

Needless to say when their dance set came to an end all eyes in the ballroom were still on them. Although no one heard Ned whisper to her how enchanting he thought she looked, before he released her hand. Sophia sensed his frustration that he was obliged to leave her, which matched her own. Only noticing then that Lucy and her parents were glaring at them across the ballroom. Ned bowed low, and she watched him depart, possibly for a moment too long.

Just when Sophia felt that she couldn't bear the situation any longer and that Ned had gone again, Lady Cynthia appeared at her side and made the matter worse by remarking on how lovely she had looked twirling across the dance floor with him. Causing Sophia to feel even more confused than ever about everything. It was as if Lady Cynthia wished her association with the Duke to continue, irrespective of the gossip it was clearly causing. Nevertheless Sophia smiled gratefully at her. The Duchess had nothing but kindness in her heart. "Is there anything you need or I can do, your ladyship," she said, quickly trying to restore herself to the position of companion where she believed she belonged.

The Duchess touched her arm gently, as a gesture of support. Secretly thrilled that her meddling had resulted in this. "No, thank you, my dear. It was enough for me to see Ned and you dancing, and enjoying each other's company. I hope to have the opportunity of seeing it many more times," she said, trying to hide her excitement as she looked pointedly at Sophia. So that she was left in no doubt whatsoever that if her relationship with the Duke did develop into a romance, they would have his mother's support and blessing.

Not knowing what to make of this revelation which was completely unexpected, the rest of the evening passed in a blur. Whilst she tried not to lose sight of Ned, and at the same time, stop her eyes from searching for him. As a result, feeling completely exhausted, Sophia couldn't help feeling relieved when she was able to retire to the privacy of her bedchamber to be alone again with her thoughts.

Chapter 27

Sophia woke up with a start. It was even earlier than usual, just before dawn, and she had been in the middle of a nightmare. Ned had told her to leave Carlfield house immediately. He had discovered her true identity, and was very angry that she had dared to be so deceitful, also that his mother would now be hurt. She was standing on the path outside the front door which Jenkins had slammed, after throwing her bag onto the path. Jimmy was for some reason laughing, and dancing a jig around her when she opened her eyes.

She knew that it couldn't be true, as soon as the memory of dancing with the Duke last night came back to her. How Ned had talked to her as if he was genuinely interested in her opinion on books, and most importantly, would value it. A tear slid down her cheek when she realised that this had reminded her of her conversations with Owen, and how she might not see him again. He was going to borrow Mary Shelley's Frankenstein for her from the circulating library, before Lucas told her she was to be married. What on earth was she going to do? At this rate she could end up losing everyone she loved. Hannah and Owen had already gone. They couldn't even write to each other. Whilst Edward and Lady Cynthia probably wouldn't be prepared to see her again when they did find out what she had done.

After receiving Hannah's letter and thinking constantly about the dilemma she was in, Sophia had by this time convinced herself that all of this was true. How could it not be? She was even dreaming about it happening. Someone would eventually recognise her, she was certain of it. Even though Ned had feelings for her, which would ordinarily have been wonderful, how would he feel if he was to discover that she was actually betrothed to the vile Lord Dilley? He would assume that a courtship had taken place between them, even worse with her consent. The whole situation was impossible, and as the sun broke through the sky Sophia decided to go for a walk. Hoping that the fresh air would help calm her thoughts, and the headache which was threatening to begin.

Wrapping a shawl around her shoulders, she made her way downstairs then outside through the kitchen door. She reached the rose garden without realising she had walked there. Her thoughts were still in turmoil. The shawl had reminded her of Lady Cynthia's kindness, even when she barely knew her, during the carriage ride from London. Whereas now it was as if she had intended for Sophia to become part of the Carlisle family all along. She began to sob when she thought of how badly she had treated her in return. Especially since it was as if the Duchess had become like a mother to her.

Sophia was startled by the sound of footsteps approaching the rose garden. Realising how foolish she had been in wandering about the grounds of the house on her own, at such an early hour. She felt afraid, not knowing who else might be there. Imagining it could be an intruder, she looked quickly around to find a hiding place but there wasn't anywhere. When she saw Edward approaching her she sighed in relief, as she quickly dried her eyes and tried to calm her heart. Feeling embarrassed then that he had discovered her in such a state.

The Duke looked deeply into them. "I am glad that I have found you here in my favourite place, although I hope I didn't alarm you," he said, gently with concern. It was impossible for him not to notice that she had been crying but which she didn't try to explain. How could she? To do so would mean revealing her secret, and Ned in any event had carried on speaking. Unable to contain his feelings any longer.

"Sophia, I have a confession to make," he said, earnestly. "I have always wanted to marry for love, just as my parents did." He hesitated for a moment when he saw the surprise on her face. Believing that she must have been expecting a proposal from him when clearly now she hadn't been. Nevertheless it had taken him most of the night to find the courage to do this, so as far as he was concerned there really was no turning back.

Whereas, unknown to him, Sophia had been afraid he was about to tell her that he had been aware of her deceit for some time, and couldn't hide it any longer. However that obviously wasn't the case at all when he continued. "From the moment we met I have been unable to stop thinking about you." Ned stepped closer to the bench, and reached for her hand.

Sophia gasped when he said, "I can no longer deny my feelings. I have fallen in love with you. I can only hope that you feel the same way about me."

With her heart racing Sophia looked into the face of the man she loved, and was still desperately afraid of losing. The situation couldn't possibly go on any longer, not now, without her telling him the truth. "My dearest Ned, there is something you should know about my past before you say any more," she said, wishing with all her heart that she didn't have to tell him about her betrothal to Lord Dilley.

"No, I will not hear it! The past doesn't concern me, only now. This very moment when I need to hear you tell me, Sophia. Can you, or do you feel the same way about me?" He said, feeling as if the world was standing still. Until his heart would surely burst with happiness when he heard her reply.

Miss Sophia Barlow had said softly, but distinctly, "yes, I am in love with you!"

As soon as she said the words he wished to hear, which would change both of their lives forever, the Duke of Carlfield dropped down on one knee and proposed to her.

Whilst Sophia couldn't believe what she had done. She was already betrothed to another man, but if she didn't accept Ned's offer now she might well lose him which would certainly break her heart. The remnants of the nightmare she had woken from not so long ago returned to her, and without thinking any further about what she was doing she said, "yes!"

Ned's arms were around her again, but this time his lips were also on hers. It was the sweetest moment in her entire life, and later, she was so glad that Lord Dilley had never managed to get around to their first kiss. He meant nothing at all to her. Whereas Ned was everything.

Chapter 28

A short while later, Edward and Sophia joined the Duchess as she was about to go into the breakfast room. They had walked back to the house side by side, and arm in arm. When the Duke told her that this was where she belonged, and nothing would part them now, it left Sophia with mixed feelings. Although she obviously didn't want to leave his side, she was worried at first that Lady Cynthia didn't know about their betrothal. She might learn from one of the servants that they had been walking through the garden unchaperoned, and in such close proximity to each other.

Ned had grinned at her then in a mischievous way, so that Sophia could see how fun loving he was under the serious demeanour he usually showed to the world. He told her that she wouldn't need to worry about anything from now on. He would care for her, protect, and love her. Whilst Lady Cynthia would shortly hear the news directly from them, before any gossip had the opportunity to reach her ears. He was certain that she would be delighted. Given the hints she had dropped earlier, about this happening.

Sophia was unable to contain her delight on the one hand, regarding her close proximity to Ned which she had craved for so long, but at the same time she fully realised that their happiness could be short lived. Depending on the reaction she received from Ned and his mother to what she still had to tell them about her past. All of which was making her feel anxious, and Edward couldn't help noticing how ill at ease she looked. He attributed this to her shy disposition, also the recent change in her status which she would no doubt still be coming to terms with. Knowing of no reason why he should regret making a marriage proposal to her. Only that they still had so much to discuss about the future, and of course their wedding.

As he had anticipated it was easy to see how thrilled Lady Cynthia was that they had come in from the garden with their arms linked, since this could presumably only mean one thing, and she smiled broadly at them both. As they turned the corner of the passageway, Ned was also talking to Sophia quite animatedly about his latest project on the estate, which to the Duchess' knowledge he had never done before. Essentially concerning the improvements to the tenants' cottages he had in hand, to which Sophia seemed to be listening very carefully so as not to miss a single word of it. Cynthia's heart went out to them both. They made such a wonderful couple. They even looked right together. So much so that it almost felt wrong for her to interrupt them, and announce that they were just in time for breakfast.

After they had sat down Edward smiled at Sophia then his mother, and said, "I have an important announcement to make before breakfast is served. Mama, I know you'll be delighted when I tell you that Sophia and I are betrothed."

For a brief moment silence filled the room, before Cynthia said, "I can't begin to tell you how glad I am, and that you have finally come to your senses, Ned. My biggest fear was that you were going to make the greatest mistake of your life by asking for Lady Lucy's hand in marriage, and not Sophia. That would have been insufferable!" She turned to Sophia then, and with tears in her eyes told her that Ned couldn't have made a better choice in finding a wife.

Edward had to keep his own emotions under control when the Duchess went on to say that his father would have been very proud of him. Smiling even more broadly through her tears of joy, she revealed that she had been longing for Sophia to become her daughter. Pulling her gently into a maternal embrace, before she kissed her forehead gently. "I can't wait for Ned and you to be married," she said, warmly. When she felt Sophia's shoulders shaking, the same as Edward had done, she thought that this was simply a reaction to what had happened. There was so much for all of them to take in, and it had all happened very quickly. She never once imagined that this nervousness came from fear.

Meanwhile Sophia was feeling overwhelmed. She had even had her first kiss, and how wonderful that had been. She still couldn't believe Lady Cynthia would officially become her mother. In that particular moment, she knew that however much Ned didn't wish to listen to her revealing her secret, she immediately had to do it. She glanced at him, and couldn't help smiling when she saw the way he was staring at her with love in his eyes. This really was the best thing that had ever happened to her. Nevertheless after taking a deep breath, and without any further hesitation, she said that there was something important they needed to know. Unfortunately she was unable to say any more, because Jenkins came into the breakfast room to announce the unexpected arrival of the Earl and Countess of Duxbury who were accompanied by Lady Lucy.

Cynthia frowned at the intrusion so early in the morning, and that they had arrived without an invitation from her. Complaining loudly of their visitors' apparent lack of good manners. Whilst Edward recalled then that he was supposed to be giving Howard his answer today, regarding whether or not he would be asking him for Lucy's hand in marriage. He was however as surprised as his mother by the Earl's arrival at such an early hour, and that he had brought his family with him. Surely Howard didn't wish to prompt him on the issue? If so it was highly impertinent, since the Duke had given his word that he would have a reply today. Alternatively if he had wished to ask for Lucy's hand in marriage, the Earl surely wasn't expecting him to make the proposal this morning, and that was why he had brought his wife and daughter with him? In his opinion, and still not knowing why his lordship regarded the matter as urgent, he couldn't help but think that Howard had lost his senses either way.

Whereas Sophia was left to sigh inwardly, that their arrival had prevented her once again from being able to reveal the truth. She certainly couldn't say anything now! It was a private matter which wasn't for anyone else's ears. Nevertheless, feeling quite euphoric by what Ned had just told her and a little light headed by the need to eat her breakfast, Lady Cynthia welcomed their unexpected guests and gestured to them to take a seat. She smiled when she said that she had some wonderful news to share. After a brief pause, while the Earl and his family looked at her in anticipation, she said that she was very excited to be able to announce that Edward and Sophia were betrothed. They had still to discuss the details of the wedding, but would no doubt be doing that later today.

Sophia was completely taken aback by this. Not realising the extent of Lady Cynthia's impetuous and independent nature, she had assumed Ned would make the announcement when he was ready. However she was even more surprised when Lucy and her father both smiled, as they congratulated Ned and her. Since this was the very last thing she would have expected them to do. Making her feel very uneasy. Something wasn't quite right about this, and she had no idea what it was! However it wasn't long before she found out. The sound of shouting was by this time coming from the hall.

Sophia felt chilled to the bone, and more than a little afraid, when Lucas pushed past Jenkins to force his way into the breakfast room. Her brother was clearly in a foul temper, and extremely angry. He looked around the table, and pointed at her with an unpleasant sneer on his face as soon as he saw her, in the same moment as Edward rose to his feet.

Chapter 29

"Ah, there you are, Sophia, my dear sister! You have a lot of explaining to do, and you won't have Owen to hide behind this time!" Lucas said, as she very quickly cringed from him. Afraid that he would on this occasion walk across the room to strike her. Given the extent of his anger, and apparent lack of restraint. Edward was however quick to act. Noticing how afraid Sophia was of this man who seemed to be her brother, presumably an older one judging by his face. What on earth had she done to cause him to react in this way? Whatever it might be he was not prepared to stand back and allow this to continue, and he quickly stood in front of her. So that she would be out of reach of Lucas.

Sophia could feel everyone staring at them when Edward moved forward to protect her. "You, Sir, will calm down. I will not tolerate such appalling behaviour," he said, firmly to Lucas. "You have entered my home forcibly, made your own way into here after ignoring my butler's request for you to leave, and spoken to Sophia in a highly disrespectful manner. Miss Barlow recently consented to become my wife, so we are betrothed. Consequently it is I who you must take issue with, if that remains your intention. Most certainly, not her!"

Sophia couldn't believe that this was Ned. Her Ned, putting Lucas firmly in his place. He was magnificent! She hadn't seen this side of him before, and despite the seriousness of the situation, she couldn't believe how strong and powerful he was. Her heart went out to him. However this turned out she knew that she would be indebted to him for the rest of her life.

"And you, Sir, I assume are the Duke of Carlfield," Lucas said, sneering at Edward. "I don't know what pack of lies my sister has been telling you, but I am her legal guardian so she cannot possibly be betrothed to you. I haven't given my consent to it. Also because I hasten to add, she was already promised to Lord Neil Dilley before she ran away from London. Sophia was fully aware of these circumstances, although I admit a formal announcement wasn't made until shortly after she disappeared."

Just then Sophia distinctly overheard Lucy telling her mother in a loud voice, which she had tried to pretend was a whisper by putting her hand in front of her face, that she knew all along there was something undesirable about Lady Cynthia's companion. The Duchess who was standing next to Sophia behind Edward, trying to comfort her, also heard what was being said. She patted Sophia's hand, and told her not to worry. Edward would deal with her brother, before she marched across the floor to where the Earl was seated next to his wife and daughter. Completely ignoring Lucas, she demanded that her unwanted visitors leave immediately. They had not received an invitation from her to be here, and what they were now witnessing was a family matter. Certainly not for public consumption. Howard was about to respond when he saw the set look on her face, and realised there would be little point in arguing. He had no intention of going to Edward's assistance, since he wished Sophia to leave Carlfield house with Lucas. Not remain, which is what would happen if the Duke had his way. With Sophia gone Lucy would be able to comfort him, and definitely secure a proposal of marriage.

While Cynthia was in the process of escorting Lucy and her parents out of the breakfast room, Edward turned around to look at Sophia and asked her if she was already betrothed. Tears were streaming down her face when she told him what had happened before she left London, and how she had tried to explain this to him in the rose garden earlier that morning. Running away had been her only option, to avoid a loveless marriage with a despicable man who was twice her age. It definitely wasn't a love match, and never would be. She continued shyly, saying that it was the Duke she loved. Surely he knew that! All the while hoping with all of her heart that he would believe her, and not hand her over to Lucas to be sent back to London to marry Lord Dilley.

Lucas laughed scornfully when he heard what she was saying, and interrupted her conversation with Ned. "You are an even bigger fool than I took you for, Sophia, if you believe that love still exists in marriage. It is simply an arrangement based on business deals, and the gentlemen making the right connections for the price of providing a home to a wife." While Edward's guard was down as he listened to this, Lucas moved quickly and grabbed his sister's arm, reiterating that he would have no more of this nonsense from her. He was well within his rights as her legal guardian to remove her from Carlfield house, after she had disobeyed him and ran away. He had made the long journey here to take her back to London." Much to the surprise of both Edward and Sophia, he went on to reveal that if it hadn't been for Howard's quick thinking he would have never tracked her down. Making Sophia realise why the Earl had made her feel so uneasy when he had been scrutinising her appearance.

Lucas added that the Earl of Duxbury had done business with him in the past. Just before he left London to travel back to Yorkshire Howard heard about Sophia's disappearance, and he had a description of her. When he first laid eyes on Lady Cynthia's new companion at the garden party he was almost certain that it was her, and he sent word to Lucas that he believed he had found his lost sister. What he didn't however tell Edward was that Howard had been happy to reveal her whereabouts for a fee. Or that Lucas had reluctantly been obliged to pay this, believing it made good economic sense to do so. Given that a much greater sum would be involved if the marriage to Lord Dilley went ahead, and the latter wouldn't expect him to return the bribe he had already received to arrange the marriage to his sister. To improve his chance of finding her, Lucas had broadcast her disappearance far and wide across London, and the fact that he was determined to find her. News of which had soon reached Howard's club.

Any initial doubts Edward might have had about whether Sophia ought to be sent back to her notorious brother were short lived, and easily dismissed from his mind. Mr Lucas Barlow was clearly a brute of a man! He imagined that his reprisals would be harsh to say the least, and he seriously feared for Sophia's safety if she was returned to him. All that aside, as the woman he loved, she was under his protection now. Whilst the Duke of Carlfield certainly wasn't afraid of a man like Lucas, a dishonest, and dishonourable brute! He had by this time recalled what he had heard about him, and his dubious reputation which bore witness to the fact. The possibility of the Duke being accused of kidnapping

Miss Barlow could be easily disproved, if Lucas should allege it. Not only was he paying her a good wage, but she was happy and well.

Moreover he could imagine his mother's reaction to her companion being removed from the family estate by Mr Barlow. He could see her trying to take her old riding crop to him. Not to mention the adverse reaction he would then receive from her friends, those ladies in Yorkshire who had met her, and whom he knew from Cynthia had been equally delighted to be in Sophia's company. Lucas would be a brave man indeed to take on their vitriol and the influence they exerted on the gentlemen in their families, the influential husbands and sons, many of whom had business interests in London.

No! Irrespective of all this Sophia was his responsibility now, and it was his duty to keep her safe. At the very least until she was legally twenty-one, and entitled to make her own decision regarding who she should marry. His heart sank when he realised that had been his only mistake. He had for some reason assumed, without asking her, that she had already reached this age. Without intending any insult to her, by inferring that she looked older than she actually was. Meanwhile whatever the future might now hold for a romance between them he would also personally help her, via Cynthia of course, to cut the ties with her brother.

Edward also couldn't stop his thoughts from racing through everything that had happened since he had first met Miss Sophia Barlow, which had led to him making a proposal. Including his own part in the matter. She had tried to tell him something this morning before she accepted, and to his dismay, he recalled insisting that the past held no interest for him. It was only the present moment which mattered. Even though he could never have envisaged that she would be involved in something like this. At no time however did he ever feel as if Sophia had deceived him. Only that he might not know the whole truth about her.

The Duke of Carlfield couldn't believe that this had happened. When he had finally found the woman he truly loved and wished to marry, he might lose her, on the very same morning he had proposed.

Chapter 30

When Ned looked into Sophia's eyes, he could see nothing but fear in them. Why she was afraid of being in a loveless marriage and under the control of a man who, if he was anything like Lucas, would treat her very badly indeed. The mere thought of which made him feel sick to the core. So without any further hesitation Edward Carlisle stepped forward, and demanded that Mr Lucas Barlow release his fiancee's arm immediately.

Lucas however stood his ground. "I am perfectly within my rights to demand that my sister comes with me. Lord Dilley has kindly agreed to delay travelling abroad for a few days, to allow me sufficient time to collect her and for them to be married. It is all arranged, Sir, and outside of your control. Something else which may have escaped your notice, and I am willing to repeat, is that I am my sister's guardian until she is twenty-one years of age!"

Sophia found her voice then, and said as firmly as she could, "a fine brother you have been to me, Lucas! You have even forgotten the date. I am twenty-one today. It's my birthday, and I most certainly do not consent to the marriage you have arranged with Lord Dilley. It was done for your own convenience, and what you will no doubt get from it."

Lucas' anger caused him to tighten the grip on her arm, and Sophia to call out in pain as he began trying to drag her out of the breakfast room. Despite Edward's surprise that it was her birthday and she hadn't revealed this to either his mother or himself, his own anger knew no bounds as soon as he realised that he should have reacted sooner. Due to his failure to do so he was seeing the woman he loved with all of his heart being hurt in front of his eyes. He quickly moved behind Lucas forcibly prising his fingers from Sophia's arm, as she continued to struggle. When Lucas was obliged to release her, he tried to punch Edward who was this time too fast for him and averted the blow. Further incensed, however, by seeing the bruise on Sophia's arm starting to form and her obvious distress the Duke couldn't help himself from hitting Mr Lucas Barlow as hard as he could. Before he said, "you have less than two minutes to get out of my house and off my property, or I shall have you thrown off. "

Not taking his eyes from Lucas he quickly put his arm around Sophia's shoulders to support her, as she looked near to fainting by this time. When he had helped her to sit on the nearest chair, Edward added that Lucas shouldn't even think of bothering his future wife ever again or he would face the consequences of such a rash action. He should instead go straight back to London, and inform Lord Dilley that he was calling off the betrothal, if indeed either of them still believed it existed. The expression on Edward's face dared Lucas to challenge what he had said.

However without further ado, Lady Cynthia appeared in the doorway of the breakfast room, accompanied by Jenkins and several of the footmen. Closely followed by the gardeners' boy and two of the grooms who had been in the kitchen trying to persuade Cook to give each of them a slice of cake when the commotion began. It appeared that the Duke needed assistance as Miss Barlow had been attacked by an intruder and Jimmy, whose heart was in the right place, had led the way to the breakfast room.

With his arm around her shoulders, Ned turned Sophia's face gently towards him, so that she wouldn't need to watch Lucas being escorted from the breakfast room by the large group of servants which had by this time gathered to complete the task. During which her brother struggled and attempted to escape Jimmy's vice-like grip on his arm. Causing him to receive a few extra kicks and blows as he was taken away from the house to the boundary of the estate, and told once again quite firmly by Jenkins that he must never return to Carlfield, in accordance with the Duke's instructions. Miss Barlow had also become too well liked by this time by all of them, and none of them approved of what they had heard or seen her brother trying to do. So Lucas could also expect to face their wrath if he was seen again.

Once he was out of sight, and Ned was carefully examining the bruise on her arm, Sophia asked him in a quiet voice why he had stood up for her when she had behaved so badly. Deceiving Lady Cynthia and him. He removed his arm from her shoulders, glad to see the colour had returned to her cheeks, and reached for hand. "I did it because I am in love with you, and although I should have listened to you trying to explain all of this to me which I deeply regret, I stand by what I said this morning before you agreed to be my wife. The past doesn't matter, only the present."

He hesitated for a moment before continuing since he was unused to talking about his own feelings. "I also have my secrets, Sophia." Seeing the look of alarm on her face he quickly told her about Joey, and why he hadn't been able to marry his best friend's sister after his death. I should have been there with him. We did everything together," he said, sadly. "So you see, all of us have something in our past which we may not always get around to telling other people."

He was staring tenderly into her eyes when Cynthia came back into the room, and coughed loudly to announce her return before saying that she would have run away too, if she had been in Sophia's position. It must have been truly awful. She smiled at both of them, and said that she would arrange for the maid to bring them tea. Maybe ask Cook to send up their breakfast now. Leaving Sophia and Ned alone again.

Having barely heard the Duchess' voice or known she was there, Sophia felt her heart thudding inside her chest when Ned drew her closer to him, and she heard him say that he couldn't wait to be able to call her his wife. The matter was sealed by them with the sweetest of kisses. Leaving Sophia in no doubt whatsoever that she would be able to stay with her husband, and the woman she now thought of as the mother she had longed for. Carlfield house would truly be her new home, where she would finally be safe, as both Ned and her knew that it really would be a marriage of love.

Whilst Lady Cynthia tried to have the final word when they were eating breakfast. "After everything you have been through, Sophia, I defy any of those dreadful ladies of the ton to try to turn what has happened into a scandal. You are part of the Carlisle family now. Neither Ned nor I will allow anyone to interfere with that. You shall also soon have a title of your own by marriage, and I do hope with several volumes of your delightful poetry published. Proving to them, and anyone else who might doubt the veracity of it, that love really does matter the most."

Ned raised his teacup to toast his mother's wise words. The gesture was followed by Sophia, and all three of them realised that they now had the life they wanted. Cynthia had her daughter, whilst Ned would no longer be lonely, and Sophia had found the true love she wished for. There would also be many more adventures, with a kind and loving husband at her side.

However, it was for love to ultimately have the last word, for it had found its way into all of their hearts. Destiny had brought together those who were meant to be, once Cupid's arrows had been fired, and it had been given a helping hand by the Duchess of Carlfield.

Epilogue

It soon became clear to Edward why Howard had been so keen to promote his marriage to Lucy, and what a lucky escape he had. After the Earl of Duxbury had been obliged to file for bankruptcy, which he didn't obviously wish to do since this could also mean facing a stay in the local debtor's prison. Along with the likelihood of his honour, and reputation, being tarnished irrevocably. It occurred to Edward that once again he had a lot to thank his mother for. The outcome of all this, and three weeks ago on the morning he had proposed to Sophia, was down to the Duchess' insistence all along that he should marry for love. All the little hints she had dropped about Lucy not being the one for him, but Sophia would be once they had met her. Whilst Howard had presumably been hoping that Edward would settle his debts after he was betrothed to Lucy, to avoid being associated with a scandal which his future father-in-law had unbeknownst to him been about to bring to his door.

Lady Amelia and Lucy were obviously distraught by their change in circumstances, since it meant that they would find it difficult to take part in polite society again, due to the reaction of the ton to the Earl's disgrace. Needless to say they were also desperately worried about their future prospects. Neither of them had any money of their own or had worked in the past. Nor could they as yet countenance taking on a paid position as a governess or ladies' companion, as Sophia had done. In Lucy's mind there also remained a sense of disbelief that Edward had preferred a servant to her.

Ned kept his promise to Sophia that she would never have anything to be afraid of again, especially not from her older brother. Although Owen never once complained or divulged exactly what had happened after she left London, he did discuss it with the Duke on the understanding that it wasn't to reach his sister's ears. Admitting only that he had suffered considerably at Lucas' hands, especially after Lucas' return from Yorkshire. Fortunately Sophia had shared her fear with Edward that this might well be the case, and he informed his future brother-in-law as quickly as he could that he was able to offer him an excellent position in his own business. Edward and he soon became the best of friends. This also ensured that Owen had the prospect of becoming a wealthy man in his own right, so could marry for love. Instead of having to pursue the more humble career Lucas had in mind for him at a country parsonage, where his prospects remained uncertain.

Hannah and Owen became regular visitors to the old dower house which was on the Carlfield estate. Sophia had moved into it temporarily until Ned and her were married, and she had been accompanied by Effie. Then Amy, after Edward arranged for her fare to be paid, and she had travelled to them from London. She would be employed initially as a house maid with two of the others from the big house, as it was known by the servants, then train alongside Effie to be a lady's maid. If she wished to return to London after that to be close to her family again the Duke said that he would pay her return fare, and do his best to secure employment for her which would be much better than her earlier position in Lucas' house. This was after Sophia told him how Amy had helped her to escape, and before that whenever she could, so Ned felt indebted to her.

However, as soon as he saw how much Sophia valued her friendship with the maid and learned that Amy had given her own mother's address as a place where she might hide when both of them had been afraid of repercussions from Lucas and his vile temper, Edward extended his initial offer to her brothers. They would also have employment in his business, if they wished to. Enabling the whole family to relocate to Carlfield. One of the tenants' cottages had recently become vacant. It would be theirs if they wanted it, and they did. Unable to believe the unexpected kindness which the Duke of Carlfield had extended to their sister, and themselves.

Neither Edward nor Owen knew exactly what transpired with Lord Dilley after Sophia announced that she was twenty-one so free of Lucas' guardianship, and Edward had told him quite categorically that he intended to marry her. Except that Lord Dilley had left for the continent not long after Lucas returned to London. Two men had apparently set upon Lucas a few nights later on the banks of the Thames. It was foggy, and he was trying to stop them from stealing his money. It seemed that he had fallen backwards, and hit his head on a rock in the tussle which ensued. He died from the injuries he sustained.

As Lucas' surviving male heir Owen inherited his brother's considerable estate, and with Ned's assistance, he used part of his fortune to help the poor of the parish in London where they had lived. He wished to give some of the money to his sister, but Ned didn't want Sophia to take it due to him having more than enough money to look after his mother and them. Although they were grateful to Owen for the offer, and his belief that she should have part of the inheritance. Since Lucas had stolen the money which Papa had left in trust for her and making her life much poorer than it should have been.

A few weeks later Edward and Sophia were married in an intimate ceremony, surrounded by close friends and family. The small church in the south wing of Carlfield house was the perfect venue. Being relatively private, and the place where most of his ancestors had been married. Under Cynthia's direction the gardeners had gathered a multitude of flowers from around the estate, and the church was decorated beautifully with them. Especially the roses Sophia loved, and which still reminded her of her mama.

Sophia told Cynthia and Edward that she thought it was like being married in a wonderful garden. Whilst being under the watchful eye of his ancestors, as she walked through the house on Owen's arm with Lady Cynthia. After leaving her bedchamber and a tearful Florence and Effie, who were overwhelmed at being able to help her get ready in the finest wedding dress they had ever seen. The seamstress and her assistant had worked many extra hours so that it would be finished on time. Disappointing several of the ladies of the ton who had insisted that they wished to have new ball gowns made for them immediately.

Sophia was delighted to have Hannah and her parents at the ceremony. The two young women were excited about being together again, especially in Sophia's bedchamber when she was putting on her wedding dress. Hannah told her that she thought Edward was exceedingly handsome, a perfect gentleman, and was thrilled when she learned how he had dealt with Lucas. Hannah admitted shyly then, that Owen and her had fallen in love. Sophia said that it made the day even more perfect than she had thought it could be, as she hugged her best friend.

All of them attended a wedding breakfast hosted by Lady Cynthia, again at Carlfield house. Sophia's belongings had been moved back to the big house earlier that morning by the footmen, where she would now be living as Edward's wife. Lady Cynthia had initially said that she would live in the dower house after their marriage, but neither Sophia nor Edward had wanted that to happen. She had become more forgetful, and frail. Despite Ruth having returned as her companion, once her mother was fully recovered, they had no desire to see her leave them.

Ned and his mother had also by this time had a conversation about her meddling, and both agreed that in this instance the end had justified the means. However the Duchess had taken the opportunity to remind him that it was her duty as his mama to ensure his future happiness, which he accepted graciously with a smile. She had also stopped doing it once they were betrothed. As she said herself she wished to be left to her own devices then, with Ruth's admirable assistance, raising funds to help the poor and needy.

However Lady Cynthia helped considerably in persuading the rather more reluctant ladies of the ton to accept her daughter-in-law. Reminding them whenever the opportunity arose that she now had a title of her own, and had been presented to Queen Charlotte when she was a debutante. Her Majesty hadn't taken issue with Sophia being a merchant's daughter, so why did they think they had the right to do so? Mostly though, even the most belligerent of mamas couldn't fail to deny the love which shone in both Ned and Sophia's eyes when they looked at each other. No one could deny the goodness in that, or suggest any impropriety. Love had won the day! Also it had to be said, Lady Cynthia. Whenever it was necessary for her to remind anyone of it she staunchly maintained that it was solely a family matter whom her son had married, and if she had given her approval to it following Queen Charlotte's example then no one had the right to object.

The ladies of the ton became grateful to receive an invitation to any of the balls, soirees, and other events she arranged jointly with Sophia. Having soon discovered that being excluded from them was far worse than accepting Edward's new wife, who really was quite charming once you got to know her, and did of course have her own title now. The gentlemen in their lives had also played an important part in persuading them that this truly was for the best since they wished to continue doing business with the Duke and Owen as well, who was about to marry Lady Hannah.

Extended Epilogue

Two years later... Edward and Sophia were happily married, and their daughter had been called Constance, after Sophia's late mother. Edward no longer travelled, unable to bear being parted from his family, and they spent most of their time in residence at Carlfield house.

Several volumes of Sophia's poems had been successfully published and it no longer filled her with dismay when she read her poems aloud to an audience, still under the watchful eye of her mother-in-law and husband.

And Lady Cynthia? She couldn't be happier. When Ned did occasionally tease her about her earlier meddling she denied it, telling him that he was being preposterous. While the truth was the Duke would never forget, or cease to be grateful for, the part she had played in him being able to marry Miss Sophia Barlow... For love.

The End

Printed in Great Britain
by Amazon